HANGMAN'S TIDE

JOHN BUXTON HILTON

CHARTER/DIAMOND BOOKS, NEW YORK

This Charter/Diamond book contains the complete text of the original edition. It has been completely reset in a typeface designed for easy reading, and was printed from new film.

HANGMAN'S TIDE

A Charter/Diamond Book/published by arrangement with the estate of John Buxton Hilton

PRINTING HISTORY
St. Martin's Press edition published 1975
Charter/Diamond edition/August 1990

ISBN: 1-55773-378-3

Charter/Diamond Books are published by The Berkley Publishing Group,
200 Madison Avenue, New York, New York 10016.
The name "Charter/Diamond" and its logo
are trademarks belonging to Charter Communications, Inc.

PRINTED IN THE UNITED STATES OF AMERICA

10 9 8 7 6 5 4 3 2 1

For
Rebecca

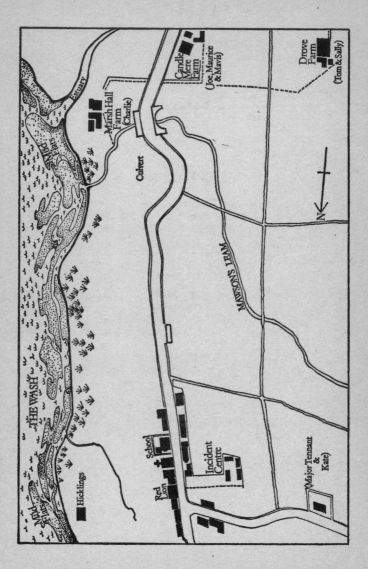

The Margerums

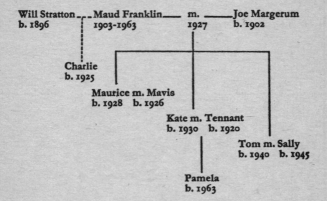

Will Stratton ---- Maud Franklin —— m. —— Joe Margerum
b. 1896   1903-1963   1927   b. 1902

Charlie
b. 1925

Maurice m. Mavis
b. 1928   b. 1926

Kate m. Tennant
b. 1930   b. 1920

Tom m. Sally
b. 1940   b. 1945

Pamela
b. 1963

·1·

FOR NEARLY AN hour they had driven past nothing but fields, flat and rectangular, no hedges or fences, every now and then a barred gate, lonely and skeletal, seeming to mark a boundary between nothing and nothing. Then one caught sight of the water in the dike, peat-brown, stagnant among the rushes. Sometimes there was a house-front, affluent and Georgian, with a cluster of barns and an avenue of limes or poplars. Occasionally there was something prosperous and modern in the Danish style, in contemporary brick, with low-pitched roofs and mansard windows. Scarcely ever did they see a sign of human activity: an occasional farmer's car, driven leisurely along the empty roads, a laborer sawing logs in a yard. No one was in the fields. The soil was heavy and sodden with green winter. Orchards were tidy, immobile and leafless. Thin drills of wheat, sown last autumn, stretched away into the mist.

"A murderer out here, Shiner, ought to be able to plead the environment in partial provocation."

"Perhaps he will, sir."

"The sea must be over there."

"It must be somewhere."

According to the map they were within a few hundred yards of the edge of the Wash. But visibility was down to the length of a football pitch, and for all they could see, they might have been in the middle of a continental plain.

"I reckon that's the sea-wall, Shiner."

"And I reckon it's a potato-clamp, or else another pile of swedes."

"Sugar-beet, Shiner!—Get it right!—They'll think we're ignorant, else."

Then suddenly there was activity ahead of them: police vehicles, one of them a dog-van, parked on the verge.

Kenworthy swerved into the edge, shoving out the clutch and stopping them ludicrously abruptly with the hand-brake. His battered old green Anglia knocked over a traffic-cone—deliberately. A constable in a flat cap came up to remonstrate. There were times when the Superintendent got a kick out of simply being Kenworthy. He lowered the window and said his name.

"Yes, sir. Good afternoon, sir."

Already the constable was easing up his personal radio from under his lapel, pulling out the aerial between finger and thumb.

"You can put that bloody thing away. They don't need to know I'm here yet. If the word gets around, I'll know who's to blame."

"Sir."

They were parked almost over a culvert. Kenworthy got out and stood on the edge of the water-course. The cold was withering and the moist air seemed to seep in seconds through coat collars and scarves.

"This is what you call Mawson's Leam?"

"Yes, sir."

The stream flowed under the metalled road. On the seaward side it ran under an arch through a grassy mound. The brickwork was weathered and overgrown in places by clumps of reed.

"This must be the old sea-wall," Wright said. "That bank on the other side of the turnips will be the new one."

"Thank you, Shiner. You're a great comfort to me. And they're not turnips. Let's take a gander."

They slopped through wet grass, skirted a bog too deep for progress, and peered into the archway.

"Does it look three hundred years old to you, Shiner?"

"Could be."

"Brilliant! And so careful, too. And those grooves down there: do they date from the seventeenth century, or were they made the day before yesterday?"

They went on their hands and knees in the damp vegetation.

"The day before yesterday, sir—give or take an hour or so."

"Correct. And why so sure?"

"No green muck in them."

"Algae, Shiner, algae—where are your manners?"

Kenworthy got to his feet and looked at the uniformed constable, who was hovering with the discretion of a butler.

"So this is where they hanged the Dutchman?"

"That's what they say, sir."

"And do you believe that yarn?"

"I don't believe it had anything to do with what happened yesterday."

"Keen thinking, Constable. Neither do I—since the events happen to be three centuries apart in time. So why should anyone try to make us think it had?"

"Someone with a whimsical turn of mind, so to speak, sir."

"Whimsical lot around here, then, are they?"

"Must be a whimsical type who'd rig up a contraption to stretch the neck of a woman in her eighties."

Kenworthy led them out along the edge of a field of roughly harrowed clods. It was heavy going; great lumps of earth clung to their heels. They clambered up the wet bank of the sea-defenses and looked eastward across the marsh. They strained their ears for the sound of the sea, but what they heard might have been no more than the rustle of sedge and the lapping of pools left by the tide. It was impossible to tell where lay swamp and where firm earth, for the tangle of winter-dead grasses and the vagaries of dead ground combined to form the perfect camouflage. And distances were deceptive: out on their right an officer taking long awkward strides in the wake of a tracker-dog cut a surprisingly small figure.

"How long have you been on the scene, Constable? Were you here when she was found?"

"No, sir. I came in with the first reserves."

"So you didn't see her cut down?"

"No, sir."

"But you did see the thing that was used as a scaffold?"

"I saw it, sir—but not to examine it closely. The C.I.D.—"

"Of course. It was a sort of floating hangman's drop?"

"That went down with the tide, sir."

"And that's how they hanged the Dutchman?"

"So the story goes."

Kenworthy went back to his car. Two saloons of sight-seers had moved in and parked across his bows.

"If you lot would care to drive on about three miles into the next village, you'll find a mangled rabbit that I ran over. It'll give you a much bigger thrill than anything you'll find here."

And then they were running into the heart of Mawson's Drove End, a village that was little more than two rows of parallel cottages on either side of a dead straight highway. The Early Perpendicular of the church was worthy of a mention in the Norfolk Guide, and so were the Tudor chimneys of the Rectory—but Kenworthy and Wright paid no heed to either. Kenworthy braked—more soberly this time—under the wall of the school playground. Already the lights were on behind the class-room windows, and he nodded his satisfaction that mothers were already beginning to congregate to take their offspring home.

They went in through the cloak-room porch, with its white-painted brick walls and its rows of bobbed woolen caps and mufflers. Kenworthy tapped formally on the Victorian gothic door and Wright followed him up the aisles between the children's tables.

It was an ancient room—the date on the outside wall was 1840—and the windows were so high that neither child nor adult could be distracted by a sight of the outside world. But the furniture was modern. Chairs and tables gleamed with the yellow newness of kiln-dried beech. A table in a corner was laid out with mathematical equipment: gaily painted trundle-wheels, plastic polyhedra and surveyors' chains. The walls were pinned with paintings in primary poster colors.

"Gwen, Susan—chairs for the gentlemen—"

The headmaster was in his early sixties: thin gray hair, close cropped in barrack fashion, and he carried no suggestion of fat. The weariness about his eyes was the product of the last few weeks, not of a life-time.

"No need for me to ask who you are. I'm relieved to see you. And that goes for the whole of Mawson's Drove."

"Not the whole of Mawson's Drove," Kenworthy said. "There's one man who won't echo your sentiments."

And all the while, his eyes and Wright's were scanning the children's faces.

"But we got here too soon, Mr. Heathcote—we can wait till—"

"Two minutes to go. I daren't let them out too soon, because of the traffic. If somebody's mother happened to be late—"

Kenworthy's eye had now lighted on the same child as had Wright's, and Heathcote showed by a movement of his head that he had caught the significance of it. All three of them instantly engaged their attention elsewhere.

The girl would be about seven, gleamingly washed and a little too fat for her age, and she was concentrating fiercely on producing a swan by the art of Japanese paper-folding. She was blonde, her hair tightly drawn and clipped at the back with a tortoiseshell slide. Her clothes were immaculate—a red jumper and a gray skirt, whose shop-bought newness set her apart from the others in the class.

Then the door of the school's only other class-room opened and the infants filed out, accompanied by their teacher, in single file towards the cloak-room. And every face was turned as it passed, to stare at the detectives. A small boy stumbled against a desk, not looking where he was going. Heathcote spoke to his own class.

"Finish what you're doing. Put your things away."

And it was all so quickly done that they were ready to go for their hats and coats as soon as the last of the infants was through the room.

"I didn't think, when I saw Cynthia Merridew come through that door on Monday morning—"

"But your troubles started several weeks before that, didn't they, Mr. Heathcote?"

"You mean Pamela—"

"Let's talk about her first, shall we?"

The headmaster, freed from his pupils, brought out his pipe and tobacco-pouch. Kenworthy did the same.

"I don't think, Superintendent, that you'll find any connection between Pamela Tennant and what happened to Miss Merridew."

"No?"

Kenworthy waited for silence to force the initiative on Heathcote.

"I'm sure of it," the headmaster said at last.

"Was it something else, then, that brought Miss Merridew into the village?"

"It brought her into the village, certainly. But it didn't choke her to a slow death in Mawson's Leam."

"Tell us about Pamela."

Heathcote sucked the flame from his match over the well-packed bowl.

"It's happening often enough in schools these days—too often by far. It's my good fortune that it's the first time in forty-three years—a quarter of a century at this very desk—that it's ever happened to me. The Tennants moved into the village last summer. The father's an ex-Major. Stickler for his title. You can see at a glance that he's the sort who'd look for trouble whatever community he moved into—"

He paused for Kenworthy to put a specific question, but Kenworthy did not oblige him.

"He didn't like my school. On her second morning, the postman brought—he didn't give it to the child to deliver—a long letter telling me all that was wrong with it. He didn't like the way we teach numbers. He thought we spent too much time playing. He would like his daughter to be set on independent work, which he suggested he might set and correct himself, if the effort were too much for us—

"Miss Burton—she's the infant mistress that you saw just now: young—but one of the best I've ever had in that room. Only she can't spell. Writes F-O-U-R-T-Y on the board, and that sort of thing. You can imagine what happened when Major Tennant got to hear of it. Then came the affair of the sandwiches—"

"Sandwiches?"

"She didn't like our school dinners, started bringing sandwiches in a packet—legitimate enough, but there's no need for it. Our canteen does a good little meal—but a few of them prefer to be loners. I didn't say much: just made a comic remark about too much carbohydrate and what would become of her figure."

"Most improper, I suppose."

"What sort of headmaster was I, to send a little girl home in tears about her personal appearance? Major Tennant had spent the prime of his life ridding Europe of the likes of me. If he'd appeared before any committee in the frame of mind in which he stormed in here, they'd have put him away, for sure. But he didn't. He started keeping Pamela at home, told his story to the press—illiterate teachers, roomful of backward children, headmaster who ridiculed a child for being just a little over-weight.''

Heathcote was beginning to work himself up. There was a certain good-natured simplicity in him that had been badly mauled in the inquisitorial outcome of all this.

''The Tennants are somehow related to the Margerums, aren't they?''

Kenworthy's knowledge seemed to startle Heathcote.

''You've obviously done your homework.''

''Only on paper, up to now.''

''Mrs. Tennant was the Margerum daughter. Sister of Maurice, Tom and Charlie.''

Kenworthy seemed satisfied. He let Heathcote continue.

''Tennant wanted the Education Committee to provide a taxi daily so that she could go to what he called a decent school. I had inspectors here, county organizers, journalists. Some of the reporters found things a bit primitive—as indeed they are. There was a lot of publicity—much of it unfair. Then they had to serve a non-attendance summons on Tennant. They only fined him a pound—but he capitulated.''

''For the child's sake?''

''His mind doesn't work like that. Otherwise none of this would have happened.''

''But where does Miss Merridew fit into the picture?''

''Nowhere and everywhere—and that's not as silly as it sounds.''

''She was active for her age?''

''An energetic woman. Sometimes a little slow to hear of things—but in her prime—''

Heathcote clearly found it difficult to do justice to her in words.

''You'd be surprised to see her again?''

''Surprised? Picture it, Superintendent. Monday morning. A new week. Dinner books. Trouble with the oil-heating. And into the thick of it walks Cynthia Merridew, twenty-one years after she's retired. I didn't recognize her, Mr. Kenworthy. It took me a minute to put a name to her face. She used to be, not exactly fat—but rotund. Now her clothes were falling away

from her bones. She used to be robust. Now she was fragile—
brittle. She reminded me of a witch—she always had reminded
me of a witch. She had a mole on her chin, with a white hair
growing out of the middle of it. When I saw her to her car,
there was a toy poodle, sitting up spry on the back seat—''

He nodded toward a child's black silhouetted poster of the
conventional figure on a broom-stick.

"I've been tempted to take that down, since this happened.
Then I thought it would be better not to draw the children's
attention to it at all.''

Wright looked at a home-made wall-map of the fields about
the village: strange local names: Black Furlong, Luke's Piece,
Dummocks. There was a short silence.

"Are you suggesting, Mr. Heathcote, that she dabbled in
witchcraft?''

"Not Cynthia Merridew. Not in the sense you mean. Not
Black Mass, or contemporary covens, or any of that filth.''

"What, then? Monkeying about with her nerves in the spot
where they hanged the Dutchman?''

Heathcote sat perfectly still. He appeared to be thinking. But
he seemed to find no new answers.

"I can only repeat, Mr. Kenworthy—not Cynthia Merridew.
It's difficult to explain. She was a curious woman—eccentric,
if you like, but exceptionally strong. And she had an odd sense
of humor, though hundreds would deny it. She looked like a
caricature of a witch—so she played on it. For her own amusement—you understand?''

He looked for support, but Kenworthy gave none.

"She even had the spot on her chin where the devil had
taken a pinch of her flesh as token of their contract. And she
had set herself up with a poodle, like a familiar spirit.''

"And she had always been fascinated by this story of the
Dutchman?''

"That and other yarns.''

Heathcote leaned backwards in his chair and hooked a book
from the case behind him.

"Cynthia Merridew, *Tales of the Marshes*. You'll find the
legend there.''

"Fill us in.''

"Charles I brought the Dutchman Vermuyden over to advise

on the drainage of the Fens. The Bedford Level was one of the key pieces of engineering."

"I remember from when I was at school."

"The project was none too popular with the Anglians. They didn't want anyone interfering with their boundaries—or with their privacy. There's a vein of obstinacy east of the Shires that goes back further than Stuart England."

"Hereward and all that—"

"As you say. And some of Vermuyden's labor-force did not endear themselves to the populace. Drunken brawls. Pregnant widows. Men set upon on their way home from taverns. Remote cottages broken into."

"It sounds like the 1970's."

"Quite. And then, as now, there was public demand for reprisals. And Vermuyden was nobody's fool. There was a case out this way where a drain-digger called Luyk—we still have a Luke's Piece—waylaid a young yeoman farmer and left him bleeding to death in the Drove, having robbed him of nothing more precious than his pocket handkerchief. It could have led to running skirmishes for months—but Vermuyden decided to give Marshland a festival instead. A jury of Dutchmen was empanelled at the *Rose* in Terrington, and Luyk was sentenced to be hanged in the way you already know about—strapped to a floating drop under the Mawson's Leam culvert. They drew every second of potential agony out of it, noosing him between tides, so that he had six hours of high water in which to say his prayers."

Kenworthy glanced at a sentence or two in the book, then seemed to lose interest in it. But Wright noticed that he was holding it in such a way as to show him the inscription on the fly-leaf.

Walter Heathcote. Sincerely. Cynthia. Summer, 1949.

"Miss Merridew was the Ministry's Inspector who used to come and look at the work of your school?"

"From when I came here in 1946 until she retired in 1950. She came roughly once a year."

"We've heard something about her reputation, Mr. Heathcote. It isn't every headmaster who'd have welcomed the news that he was to be answerable to Miss Merridew."

"And nor did I. Believe me, Superintendent, I was petrified, when they first told me. The first time she came through that door, I stood up to speak, and my voice just wouldn't come.''

"But she didn't live up to her bad name?''

"Yes and no. Miss Merridew's visits could be, and often enough they were, a catastrophe for everyone about the premises of a school. She had an eagle-eye for a fault, and once she'd found one, she saw nothing else. It didn't matter how much good you were doing in other directions—it went unnoticed—''

"The children must have loathed her.''

"Some did, some didn't. That was one of the curious things about her. I never knew her speak to a child without—well, tenderness is the only word for it. She once told me that she didn't give a tinker's cuss—there was a certain raciness about her conversation, but it was always slightly out of date—she didn't give a tinker's cuss for a soul in Education, from the Director down to a part-time cleaner—but if anyone offended a child, they'd answer to her for it. It was ironical, really, because it often just didn't work out that way. Kids have a quick intuition, and there were some who were as scared of her as I was—no matter how sweetly she spoke to them.''

"Then it seems to me, Mr. Heathcote, that you got on with her singularly well. Did she find the running of your school so efficient?''

"I was lucky, Mr. Kenworthy.''

"Is that all?''

Silence. A paper-clip lying on the table-top beside a pot of paste. A pile of Schools Broadcasting pamphlets gathering dust in a corner.

"She liked what we were doing, the first time she called.''

"And what was that?''

"I'd borrowed some vestry records, and the children were tracing their surnames back into the fifteenth century. That appealed to her immensely.''

"And, also, this was one neighborhood in which she did not want to make enemies?''

"There is an element of truth in that.''

"Because of the Margerums?''

For the second time, Heathcote was uneasy at the mention of the name.

"Others can tell you more than I can about the Margerums, Superintendent."

"I shall be asking them—as I'm asking you."

"The Margerums were a valuable contact for her: a well of folk-lore. Some of her best stories came from that source."

"Which source, Mr. Heathcote?"

"The Margerums."

"Which Margerum?"

Heathcote hesitated.

"Charlie, I suppose."

"But you don't like talking about him?"

"I can't pretend I know Charlie Margerum."

"You mean you don't want to be the first to tell me that he served a prison sentence."

"Since you know about it already—it was a long time ago, Superintendent, just after the end of the war. And the general opinion of the village has always been that he carried the can for his father and brothers."

This was precisely what Kenworthy had said about the case on their way here. But he did not repeat it now.

"Do you believe that, Mr. Heathcote?"

"I'm not in a position to judge."

"But you have observed the relationship between the brothers over the last twenty-five years."

"The Margerums keep themselves to themselves."

"And so do you, I suppose?"

"I've scarcely spoken to a Margerum once in a twelve-month."

"But Cynthia Merridew had?"

"She was on good terms with them all, as far as I know. But I don't doubt that it was Charlie who was most useful to her. He knows more about local traditions than the rest of his family together."

"So Miss Merridew's visits did not stop when she retired?"

Wright, searching Heathcote's face for every reaction, found the headmaster's uneasiness elusive. He seemed to have neither the shiftlessness nor the aggressive confidence of dishonesty, but between the extremes there was an acute discomfort—of which Kenworthy was happily conscious: and on which Kenworthy was leaning.

Heathcote had let his pipe go out. He half made to light it again, but apparently decided to answer first.

"Apart from an extended holiday abroad, she continued to come about once a year. She dropped into the school just as if she were inspecting it, glanced over the children's work—even once asked to see the register."

"You could have complained to your authority."

"Why should I? She was doing us no harm, and herself a lot of good. It was just another game she was playing. Staying in touch—stopping herself from growing old."

"And providing herself with cover for her visits to Charlie Margerum?"

There was a characteristic pause. This time, Heathcote did strike a match. And with his first puff of smoke he added, unexpectedly, "She needed that too, of course."

"For what purpose?"

"She was still writing books."

And Kenworthy suddenly relaxed. He was a consummate actor in interrogation. He could smile with his eyes without softening the remainder of his features. Wright knew the routine. It could be very effective at the stage when people were being won into the Old Man's confidence.

"You've got most of her published works, I suppose?"

"Her tales and legends. I haven't bothered with her editions of the classics. A bit above my head."

"Which classics?"

"Catullus, Martial, Petronius Arbiter."

"A bit above mine, too. So, she arrived here on Monday morning. Where did she spend Monday and Tuesday nights?"

Kenworthy had hardened his eyes again—but Heathcote was not taken off his guard.

"I've heard that your colleagues have established that she didn't stay at the *Red Lion*."

"And that's all you know?"

"That's all I know."

"Were you on Christian name terms with Miss Merridew, Mr. Heathcote?"

There was nothing to suggest that this rocked the teacher's composure.

"You're referring to what she wrote in front of the book? I saw it catch your eye."

"I do find it rather eye-catching."

"I was surprised when I saw what she had written. It was not in character. I doubt whether there was anyone outside her immediate family circle—if she had one—who ever called her Cynthia. I came to the conclusion that something must have distracted her attention, and she didn't actually finish signing her name."

"She finished writing the date underneath it," Kenworthy said.

·2·

IT WAS ALWAYS a relief to Wright when the Superintendent had finally been brought to attend to the requirements of the Incident Center. It was a paraphernalia that the Old Man hated—and a machine, incidentally, which he always handled extraordinarily well. He cupped his hand over Wright's elbow as they came out of the school yard.

"It's time we had a look at the Big Top."

Which meant that for the next half hour he would be putting on a show of irascibility, treating with contempt everything that had been organized to date. Men with tin lids full of squashed cigarette-ends would be standing sheepishly to attention. Some well-meaning county Chief Inspector, whom he wanted out of harm's way, would be saddled with the job of Camp Commandant. Kenworthy would come away laughing up his sleeve. And towards the end of the case he would go thundering back into the H.Q., barking some impossible demand, which would have the cohort running around like hens after a lump of bacon rind; and which would suddenly sew everything up.

"We certainly don't need any of this drivel this time. If ever a case was strictly within the family, this one is."

The tactical headquarters had been set up army fashion, with a radio truck and a cluster of trailer caravans in a corner of a field. Already, enough ruts had been churned up to make the going prohibitive.

They went and looked at Exhibit A, a sort of wooden bridge, some nine feet long—a little less than the span of the Leam. Its sides were built up of green painted timber, with stout supporting struts. The width of the scaffold was little more than that of an average man and the victim, with his hands behind his back, and his ankles strapped to the stanchions, would have no chance of escape until the ebb-tide released his weight to the rope. To one side were fitted rounded metal lugs of the sort commonly used to slot together the parts of an iron bed-stead, and that were obviously meant to slide down the grooves in the arch.

"You were wrong about the algae, Shiner."

"Sir?"

"The grooves are in fact three hundred years old. The green muck was scraped out of them the day before yesterday. Get this thing to Forensic. Have it taken to pieces in such a way that it can be put together again. Get them to look at the rust on the nails, and that sort of thing. I want to know when it was made—shall we say, five or six years ago? And it's obviously been put together by cannibalizing some larger, older contraption, purpose as yet unspecified. I'd like to know the approximate age of that, too—fifteen to twenty years at a guess. The chemist might be able to tell us something from the paint. Yes, Chief Inspector?"

The man saddled with all the staff work, already harassed, came forward with a neat folder.

"The full path. report, sir. The one we sent by teleprinter was only an interim job."

"Don't tell me: she was hanged twice."

"As a matter of fact, sir—"

"Ultimate death, I suppose, by slow strangulation. In neither case were cervical vertebrae broken or dislocated. But let's not be too hard on Chummy over that. It happened in judicial executions more often than the Home Office would ever care to admit. So. She was hanged once, in decent privacy, and then the corpse was brought down to the water's edge for a theatrical send-off."

"That's what the pathologist thinks."

"And supports, I've no doubt, by all sorts of revolting detail about the abrasive effect of rope pulling against flesh already dead. Scar the color of a crushed ripe blackberry."

The Chief Inspector looked suitably impressed.

"Bloody obvious, I'd have thought," Kenworthy said, and Wright reflected that this looked like being one of his lucky cases.

"Shiner, I'm going to be tied up here for the next few

minutes. Start going the rounds. Go to the Tennants first. You know what we're looking for. Then go and chat up the Margerums. I'll pick you up somewhere in mid-stream. Leave Charlie till last. He interests me.''

So Wright considered that he was getting some of the luck, too, escaping into the open world, while the whirlwind winnowed chaff from the temporary office center. He stood for a moment in the village street, looked the length of a row of red-bricked cottages, glanced at the thatch of the pub, the Rectory chimneys already fading into half-light. Then he set out for the interview that appealed to him least among the evening's prospects.

It was a long and messy walk to Major Tennant's home—Mawson's Drove's specimen of East Anglian Danish. Basically a large bungalow, a loft window had been thrown out of the roof. A garage, with up-and-over doors, and wide enough for two cars to stand side by side, was an extension of the house, which stood in about an acre of ground: an orchard behind, space for a lawn, levelled, but as yet neither seeded nor turfed.

Wright prepared himself for the onslaught: the insolent Sandhurst drawl, the complacent contempt for the dim-wittedness of the force, a thinly veneered disinclination to be questioned by a mere sergeant, perhaps even a supercilious guess at Wright's own military record—he had been a National Service lance-jack.

It was not Tennant that Wright was afraid of—it was himself. One of these days he was going to break through and lash out at one of these jumped-up bastards—as he could easily picture Kenworthy doing. Only when you were a Superintendent, it was a little easier to snick the repercussions through the slip-field.

He pressed the bell-push with its permanent red glow, and a muffled two-tone chime sounded somewhere in the house. He pictured the hall, with its imitation highwayman's pistols in patent brass, its miniature warming-pan, its engine-turned wrought iron and its mass-copied Tretchikoff.

Instead, the door opened on a fitted hair-carpet of subdued tone and an atmosphere of mellowed oak, derived mainly from an antique settle and an ancient vestry coffer, on which the telephone stood. There was an abstract in oils on the wall, not readily comprehensible, if indeed it were meant to be, but at least original. Wright, conditioned as he was to making overall assessments first, and analyzing them afterwards, was conscious of the comfortable and the genuine in unpretentious combination. There was a surprising absence of *Kitsch*; the things about the home were unspectacular, authentic—and put to everyday use.

He had a similar feeling about the woman who opened the door to him: good-looking, in her mid-forties, she had clearly been attractive in her youth and was well cared for in a non-aggressive way. Moreover, she had obviously been anticipating such a visit—which was not surprising—and led him through the house with every promise of amiable and intelligent co-operation.

Even more surprising was the impression of reasonable affability created by the man who advanced from the lounge with his hand extended: a short, spare figure in a grey woolen cardigan that sagged about his shoulders, accentuating the fleshlessness of his frame.

Major Tennant took the trouble to read the warrant card properly.

"Sergeant Wright? Yes, I'd heard they were sending Kenworthy."

"You know your Yard, I see."

"I read my newspapers. Every word in them. You have to, in my line of business. It's surprising where you can pick up ideas."

The rather-too-bonny child with the red jumper and the gray skirt was sitting at one end of a polished refectory table, over which a Fablon runner had been laid, and was painting by numbers from a box of patent oils.

"I think you'd better take your bag of tricks up to your room, Pamela. Put the electric fire on, if you're cold."

She picked up her things, and Wright held the door for her. She smiled as she passed him, but it was a disciplined courtesy, even at her age. There was no feeling behind it.

"We had her a little late in life, as you'll have gathered," Tennant said. "A little surprise, let's say—a very pleasant one, too. You'll have heard already all the stories about our little to-do—"

On a writing-table under the window stood a portable typewriter, with a half-finished, double-spaced quarto sheet and carbon in progress. Seeing the movement of Wright's eyes, the Major went over and read from the machine.

"Since you've come across me in the middle of my secret vice, you may as well wallow in the fullness of the mire. *Darling! There are things in life that make one believe in Providence.* That's Susan Shires. I do one a year under that label. As Marguerita Blair I'm doing rather better: one every three months, under contract, direct into paperback. Revolting; and very rewarding. Too early for a drink, is it? Surely you're not going to decline on grounds of duty? What's that they always say on tele? Off watch, refreshments?"

"Never off watch, sir."

Nevertheless, he accepted a whiskey; and then at once broached business.

"Did Miss Merridew call here on Monday evening?"

"She did. A charming woman—and a ghastly business— there's nothing one can say about it: or does that sound too much like a quote from Marguerita?"

"You know that she retired years ago—she had no standing in this matter?"

"Standing? Where does standing enter into it? She talked sound sense."

Wright decided to risk a shock approach.

"It surprises me to hear you say that. Her best friends wouldn't describe her as given to compromise. And your own reputation, if I may say so, sir—"

Sooner or later he had to puncture this man's charm. He waited for the explosion; but Tennant only smiled.

"Miss Merridew had talked to Pamela that morning in school, Sergeant. I was furious at first. Things had begun to settle down, and I hadn't wanted her to be reminded. However—I don't know what it was Miss Merridew said—Pamela wouldn't talk much about it. But the transformation was amazing. Suddenly there was happiness shining from her forehead. Forgive me; Susan Shires first said that."

"I'm afraid I haven't read any of the lady."

"Wise man."

"And at what time did Miss Merridew turn up?"

"Not until after supper. Pamela had just gone to bed. Trust a woman like that to think of all the details. She was just in time to join us for coffee."

"Exuding pure charm?"

"That's loaded, Sergeant—and manifestly unfair. Cynthia Merridew's charm was natural."

"You'd met her previously?"

"Never in my life."

"But I presume that Mrs. Tennant—"

Wright turned to the woman, who was sitting less than comfortably, too near the edge of one of the fire-side chairs, most of her weight taken by her elbow on the arm.

"My wife, Sergeant Wright, has been away from Mawson's Drove for many years. Hers and her brothers' lives are worlds apart."

"Are you an expert on local legend, too, Mrs. Tennant?"

She shook her head.

"I've heard of Hickathrift and Black Shuck, of course—but all this other disgusting business—"

"I know you have to ask her, Sergeant—but Mrs. Tennant isn't going to be able to help you much. Just confine yourself to bullying me."

He said it pleasantly enough.

"Pamela was desperately unhappy when we first moved here, Sergeant. Previously she'd only been to a private kindergarten around the corner. Carshalton. Small classes—only seven or eight. Individual attention. Apple of teacher's eye. Little boys who'd been taught to wipe their noses. You can imagine what a shock Heathcote's rabble was to her. And she knew she wasn't being taught anything."

"So you went hammer and tongs for Heathcote?"

Tennant poured himself another whiskey, made a gesture of offering the decanter to Wright, but did not press when Wright declined.

"Have you never made a mistake in your life, Sergeant? Have you never watched yourself being carried beyond all reason by your rage, knowing that you haven't the power to stop yourself?"

"It didn't do anyone much good, did it, sir? Pamela least of all."

"Don't rub it in, Sergeant."

Wright tried to imagine the little man in uniform, lording it on the barrack square or in the orderly room.

"To say nothing of Heathcote," Wright insisted. He had to

make this man lose his temper. "That poor devil's been nearly out of his mind."

"I know. I'm sorry. I shall do what I can for him. I've already sent him a fiver for his school fund."

Wright moved to less dangerous ground.

"Mrs. Tennant, you say, has not lived particularly closely to her family?"

"Largely Salisbury Plain and Cyprus. We have led our own life."

"But—forgive my being so personal—"

How differently might Kenworthy have handled this man? Tennant continued in his tone of man-to-man understanding, though not without innuendo.

"I do appreciate, Sergeant, that you've been briefed to pursue a line that is embarrassing you. But I assure you—you won't embarrass me."

"I was wondering why you came back here to live."

"Why not? We don't have to live in the Margerums' pockets. This excellent plot was part of Kate's patrimony. Susan and Marguerita flourish in the Norfolk soil. And there are wild fowl on the marshes. Does that dispose of our personal arrangements? And may we now move on to Charlie Margerum?"

Wright looked meaningfully at two framed photographs, post-card size, that hung flat against the wall beside the chimney-breast. One was an unposed family group, with neither focus nor composition. There was a man—a farmer in his working clothes, with one shirt sleeve rolled up higher than the other, aged between forty and fifty. Beside him was a woman, about the same age, unready for the camera, screwing her eyes up against the sunlight. There were two grown-up sons, one of them standing a little apart from the group, and a boy in his mid-teens.

"Introduce me," Wright said.

"My father-in-law—this was taken sometime in the 1950's. My mother-in-law, caught, as you see, unawares. Maurice, the middle boy, next to his mother—looks as if he might possibly be a farmer, doesn't he?"

The man, though only in his early twenties, was already beginning to look bovine: thick-set, round shouldered, his arms dangling a little in front of him.

"That's Charlie, in the rear—"

Darker-haired than the rest; brooding eyes; a scowl for the camera—though he, too, may simply have been trying not to look into the sun.

"The other's the baby of the family—Tom. I've no doubt you'll meet them all before Kenworthy lets you go to bed tonight."

"And where were you, Mrs. Tennant, when this was taken?"

"Taking it," she said simply. "And holding the camera rather less than straight."

And the other photograph was a studio cameo, taken some years previously; the same woman, though it was not easy to be sure at first sight.

"Take if off the wall, if you want a good look, Sergeant."

And Mrs. Tennant got up from her chair.

"If you'll excuse me, Sergeant—"

The portrait was a highly stylized pose. Her skin, her high forehead, gave the impression of having been vigorously scrubbed. Her shoulders were highly padded, her hair piled towards the back of her head. Her blouse and the brooch at her throat seemed to belong to an even earlier era, as if, in the 1940's, she were trying to hark back to the twenties. There was a sadness in her eyes—or so Wright thought—and he found himself comparing her expression with that of the drop-out son in the other picture.

"A handsome woman," Tennant said.

"She's been dead how long? Six or seven years?"

"That's right. An unhappy soul. With every reason—"

Wright waited for the story, but Tennant had prepared a preamble.

"You'll have heard gossip in the village."

"We haven't had time to gossip in the village—yet."

"Perhaps that's a good thing. And as I'm about the only unprejudiced outsider that you're likely to meet—"

"Do go on, Major Tennant, please."

"I'll begin at the beginning. That always solves the first of a story-teller's problems. And I'm afraid this is going to sound rather like one of my own romances. The Franklins used to own pretty well every acre and rood that was worth owning in and around this village: that's Candle Mere Farm, where the old man and Maurice still are; this little patch, and the pastures round it, which Maurice still uses for grazing, though he pays

Kate a nominal rent for them; Drove Farm, adjacent to the main holding, which young Tom farms; and Marsh Hall Farm, on the other side of the road, stretching right down to the outfall—''

''Charlie's place?''

''You have it. It all belonged to old Franklin—all bar Drove Farm, which belonged to Kate's father, Margerum senior—are you beginning to get the picture? Franklin was a gentleman of the old school; owned more than half the cottages in the village, and the amount he gave away in rents not collected is just nobody's business. But that's neither here nor there. He was away throughout the war—the Marne, the Somme, the Retreat in 1918—he saw the lot. And that was the time when his daughter, Maud, Kate's mother, was growing up. She'd be, what—oh, born about 1903, 1904—she'd be fourteen or fifteen when her father came home. And she'd been brought up as a lady. Those weren't the days when girls drove tractors—not a daughter of Thomas Franklin, anyway. She rode the lanes on summer mornings—side-saddle. There were tennis parties to which the right people came—from as far afield as Hertfordshire and the Breckland. She was, from all accounts, a soprano worth listening to. She played the cello. She read poetry—Rupert Brooke and Frances Cornford and the like, and wrote derivative stuff herself, of which her parents thought pathetically highly.

''Then her mother died, about 1922—and she turned her hand to housekeeping for her father, at which stage the dark-eyed stranger arrived in the form of—well, this is so corny, I'd use it as a plot myself, if I thought I could get away with it—a strong, silent man, black avised with smoldering eyes. He turned up one day, and knocked on the Franklins' door—and there was nothing that old Franklin wouldn't do for him. It turned out that this chap—Will Stratton—had been his batman, right through from the earliest days to the armistice. There'd been some sort of sentimental promise, if ever Will fell on evil days. And so he had—so evil that he'd almost been compelled to work for a living. He was a West Countryman, as far as I've been able to make out—Worcestershire, or somewhere like that. At any rate, he spoke a brogue that the locals found difficult to understand.''

Tennant's eyes seemed fired with a genuine hatred of the man.

"He was a blackguard. He rapidly became one of the most detested men in Mawson's Drove. He drank too much in the *Red Lion*—and he was tight-fisted in any company. He picked quarrels, and he fought dirty. He sold his master's game and eggs behind his back—birds from the breeding-pens and cartridges from the armory; as I've no doubt he flogged the old man's cigarettes and whiskey in the trenches. But Thomas Franklin was as blind as a bat to all this, it seemed. He was not a man who imputed to others motives that he didn't know himself. He'd made a promise in Flanders, and he kept it. He took Will Stratton on as an extra—and quite unnecessary—laborer. He fixed him up with a bunk-house bed in a shed where they stored apples. And Stratton was used enough to pigging it. He could have turned the place into a little paradise—but he preferred to sleep under horse-blankets, with a strip of old carpet beside his bed that had been thrown out of the house. What sort of batman he had been, we can imagine.

"Then old Franklin had a shooting accident. About 1924—well, you can take that or leave it. But I can tell you, if you try to follow that trail, you'll find that there's no spoor left. I know, because I tried to dig it up on one of my early visits. People only remember what they want to—and they forget some of that. Old Tom Franklin knew too much about guns, for my money, to fall fatally on his own. And Will Stratton knew plenty about small arms, too."

Tennant suddenly pricked up his ears, at a sound that Wright had missed. But, in the kitchen, Kate Tennant had also heard it, and they heard her race upstairs. Tennant seemed to have lost track of his narrative, and after a few seconds he excused himself and also left the room. Wright went over to read what was on the typewriter.

"I thought I had deserved better of you than this," she sighed.

The diffuse lighting fell on the soft down of her cheek.

There were other photographs of the Tennants about the room: a mess group with a regimental crest; a slight and bony-kneed cadet coxing an army eight at Henley; but nothing else of the Margerums as a family.

Tennant came back into the room, making the most of a bout of anger that seemed moderately sincere.

"It's the first time that's happened—Pamela crying. Because of what happened to Miss Merridew. She's bottled it up till now."

"If you'd rather we stopped talking—"

"It's all right. Kate's coping. Men are better out of this sort of thing. Where were we?"

"Franklin's accident."

"Yes. Well, you can imagine the effect on Kate's mother, only a couple of years after losing one parent. And after leading such a sheltered life. It wasn't what you'd call roughing it, you know, housekeeping for her father, with a house and a yard full of servants. But she had a stubborn strain. She determined to show that she could manage. And it isn't that there was any lack of offered help: the family solicitor, a batch of uncles from the fens around Ely—to say nothing of Joe Margerum, over the fence at Drove Farm, already in his twenties, and well aware what sort of a young neighbor he had.

"But Maud was as strong-willed as she was wrong-headed. Somehow or other, she let Will Stratton ingratiate himself. It wasn't long before he was more than a laborer; he became virtually bailiff. She sacked other servants right, left and center—anyone clear-sighted enough to see through Stratton, and honest enough to speak his mind. Stratton didn't give up his bunk-house bed—but he lost no time finding his way into the house—"

"And fathered Charlie?"

"And fathered Charlie."

"There was no thought of marriage?"

"God forbid. My guess is, Stratton wasn't free, anyway. I dare say he had some fouled-up nest in Worcestershire. And he wasn't slow to shake the marshland soil off his boots, either, once the junketing started giving way to responsibility. One poacher's moon, he was away. And nobody felt much like helping to go and look for him. Maud was broken—and but for Joe Margerum—"

"Who now came into his own—"

"He'd never given up hope. He'd courted her after his fashion—passively, you might almost say—for years. And he had to be patient for a while longer. Maud had a breakdown. She was away for nearly two years, and the child was cared for in the village. She ought to have had him adopted. However—sober and silenced, she came back more or less mended—and Joe Margerum completed the process. Only, when she accepted my father-in-law, he had to accept Charlie. You'll hear other versions in the village, but they won't differ in any detail that matters."

Then Mrs. Tennant brought the child into the room, eyes still red, and with a silent sob that still shook her shoulders now and again.

"I'm sorry to interrupt—but Pamela thinks she'd rather be where there are people."

"A sound idea, Mrs. Tennant. We've more or less finished, anyway."

They hadn't—but the follow up to this would need Kenworthy.

"Pamela—this is the nice detective who's come to lock up the man who did that dreadful thing."

Pamela smiled bravely and moistly.

"I'm here to do my best," Wright said.

Then Pamela turned suddenly on her father.

"I don't care what you say. I know it wasn't Uncle Charlie."

· 3 ·

THE TENNANTS LEFT the light over their porch burning until Wright was clear of the drive. He was well out into the lane before it was switched off, with a sudden finality, as if they had succeeded, at a touch of a finger-tip, in shutting themselves away from his intrusion into their lives.

The darkness was now absolute, and one of its effects was to accentuate the silence—or the noise—it was difficult to know what to call it. He stood and listened—and did not know whether there was anything to hear or not. Was there a surge of surf on a mud bank, a quarter of a mile away? Was there a splash of a pebble in a pool? If so, was it some commonplace in the life of the night—or was someone moving about, somewhere between land and sea, where there was no call for any man to be? Was there some grazing animal in the field on his landward side, breathing, moving a heavy and lethargic limb? Or was there only the emptiness of a still and enervating mist?

For seconds only, Wright dawdled. Then he brought his torch from his pocket—he was compulsively mean with batteries—and played it on the ground before him. Held directly ahead, the beam was lost in vapor less than a couple of yards in front of him, but it was enough to show him where to put his feet.

To reach the other part of the Margerum territories, he had to return through the village. There was no street-lighting. Even the bulb on the inn sign was too weak and too high to penetrate the mist. The light from curtained windows and the shafts escaping under cottage doors were scarcely visible unless his sleeve was actually brushing the house wall. He struck inland. It would be about half a mile to where two of the Margerums' farms straddled the highway.

And the horn of a car sounded in the small of his back,

almost before he was aware of the sound of engine and tires. He side-stepped, and Kenworthy pulled up alongside him, leaning over to unlock the handle of the passenger door.

"Anything?"

Wright began his story, and before he had got far, Kenworthy had pulled in again, his near-side wheels across the entrance to a gateway. He listened without interruption, the faint light from the dial-lamps playing on their faces, an irregular drip from the branches of a hawthorn falling on to the bonnet.

"So what would be your line, Shiner? Pull Charlie in, and have a go at him?"

"Give us an hour with the others first, and we'll be in a stronger position to chat up Charles."

Kenworthy had not put the question in the tone of a man wanting advice. It was not even one of those Socratic exchanges reminiscent of Wright's training days. In their last few cases he had been treating his Sergeant a lot less like an imbecile. Now he was merely using him as a baffle board for his own thinking.

"Murder is usually a fairly straightforward encounter, Shiner. By the time it's got to killing, the issue has usually fined itself down a bit. It's true that the average murderer usually makes some sort of effort to cover up—but he's usually got too much else on his mind to make a proper job of it."

"Yes, sir."

"So we mustn't expect an entertaining puzzle every time. We mustn't be disappointed if they call us out on an easy one now and then. Shiner: we might have this tied up by midnight."

He stretched out his hand towards the ignition key.

"There is one point, though. If this were your case—and your time will come, my lad, before you think you're old— would you be sending out an all-systems call for Will Stratton?"

"After all this time?"

"It could be done. At least, if we really wanted him, there'd be enough outside hope to make it worth a try. Army records. His native heath. Vestry register. Wife's maiden name. Chat up the senior citizens."

Wright answered quietly.

"In half an hour from now, sir, we shall know whether we really want him."

"And why might we want him, Shiner?"

"Because his is the sort of story that might have interested Cynthia Merridew. She too might have been digging into vestry registers and looking for former neighbors."

"Full marks, Shiner."

Kenworthy started the engine.

Candle Mere Farm was solid, spacious and sprawling—a curious mixture of homeliness and discomfort, of casual living and a certain old-fashioned rigidity of convention, of affluence mingled with mean economies. There was an open fireplace in which half a tree was burning—but one had to sit with one's knees almost up the chimney to get any benefit from it. There was an escritoire that might have been Sheraton, but it had a broken hinge and its lid, lying askew, was loaded with old copies of *The Field* and *Farmer's Weekly*. The family were watching television when the detectives came in, on a huge console model with a twenty-three inch screen; but the picture was distorted. Something simple but fundamental was wrong with the horizontal hold, yet it had apparently not occurred to anyone to turn a knob and put it right.

Joe Margerum was in his sixties, a tall man, not fleshy—not as ram-rod straight as he must once have been, no longer as quick in his movements; and presumably his eyes had once been more alert than they were now. But he still looked as if he might have the wits and the endurance to match many a man fifteen years his junior. He was wearing neither collar nor tie, and the brass stud at his throat was broken; his carpet slippers were out at the toes, and broken behind the heels—but his hair was close cut and brilliantined.

Maurice, his son, was a matured version of the young man Wright had seen in the Tennants' photograph—florid, almost shambling, slow of speech and apparently of thought—but not necessarily stupid for that. There was no spontaneity about him. He answered questions when they were put, sometimes even gave two sentences when one would have sufficed, but he volunteered nothing on his own initiative. Two or three times, at the end of a phrase, he took a side-glance at his father. The old man had probably given up some of the more active jobs about the farm, but he was clearly firmly in control of the household.

Maurice's wife was a buxom woman of about Kate Tennant's

age—but her hair-style dated from the Second World War. She wore no make-up, and was dressed for farm-house chores. It was hard to believe that these people had not expected a visit this evening—but they had done nothing to their appearance in preparation for it. Nor did they offer their callers any hospitality. Joe Margerum sat stiffly, waiting for Kenworthy to begin. Wright had no difficulty in picturing him as the passive young gallant who had patiently courted Maud Franklin.

"I want to know when Cynthia Merridew called here, where she'd just come from, how long she stayed and where she went next."

No one had yet thought of turning off the television. Maurice Margerum's eyes, as of habit, strayed towards the screen. Kenworthy rose, crossed the room and switched off the set. The silence that followed was not without a certain element of shock.

"Have you the right to do that, in a private house?" the old man asked, but Kenworthy ignored him and he did not press the point.

"I asked you a question, Mr. Margerum."

Kenworthy looked at each face in turn. Mrs. Margerum the least at ease, was nevertheless the first to answer.

"It was Monday."

"We know that."

"What time would it be now? Let me think. It would be after lunch. I generally try to put my feet up for twenty minutes."

"We've already given every possible detail to one of your colleagues," Margerum said.

"So you've had a bit of practice at remembering. Let's cut out the play-acting, shall we?"

The father took a deep breath and assumed a deliberate tone, quiet and mannerly—a man who had spent his lifetime handling his own affairs.

"Superintendent, we are all very sorry for what has happened. It was a great shock to us, and we are tired. But I do not see how we can help you. Miss Merridew, who was no more than a casual acquaintance over the years, had very little to do with us, nor we with her."

"All of which I shall be more than happy to accept, but not

on what evidence we have up to now. Now—at what time did she come here?"

The woman answered.

"About ten to two."

"How long did she stay?"

"Not half an hour. She was in a breezing hurry. She usually was."

"How long was it since you had last seen her?"

"Years. Six or seven. We've been having an argument about just when it was."

"My impression was that she made an annual visit."

"She used to. Even after she retired, for a few years. Then she went abroad—Greece, Egypt, Palestine, South Africa. Then she had an illness. We didn't really correspond—just post-cards from holidays and at Christmas time."

"So what was your friendship based on?"

Kenworthy looked directly at Maurice, and forced him to take his turn.

"You'd hardly call it friendship."

"Would it be true to say that it was a friendship with your mother, while she was still alive?"

"They enjoyed each other's company."

"Talking about what?"

"Miss Merridew was interested in old Norfolk."

"And you, as a family, could tell her a lot that she wanted to know?"

Old Margerum took up the point.

"It would be misleading to say that. We're not all experts. But Miss Merridew was a writer. She could make a lot out of a little. Hickathrift, the Norfolk giant—Shucky dogs—supposed to be messengers of death, if you come across them on the marsh. Load of superstitious nonsense. But grist to Miss Merridew's mill. We're an old Norfolk family. Things we took for granted were often interesting to her—little things—like Matty Lamp-oil—old Matt Chittleburgh, who used to sell from door to door. We filled in a lot of that kind of detail for her."

"And Luyk, the Dutchman?"

"I learned more about him from her book than I'd ever known before."

"So where did she get that story from?"

There was a moment's silence. Kenworthy swung his eyes to Maurice.

"My brother over the road goes in for such things. He knows all the old tales."

"Did Miss Merridew spend Monday night in your brother's house?"

Again they were not anxious to reply. Then father and son tried to answer together. Then Maurice left it to the old man.

"She might have; she might not. We don't know. I thought I'd made that clear to the other officer who called. What goes on across the road is not our affair."

"Your son—"

"He's not my son—"

"We won't labor that point. We know the facts. Is he a bachelor?"

"Not surprisingly."

"There's no love lost between you?"

"He lives his own life."

"He went to prison, didn't he?"

"That's over and done with."

"Does *he* think so?"

"What do you mean by that, Superintendent?"

And then, as Kenworthy pointedly refused to answer, the old man extended himself.

"If you want further information on that affair, you have access to records, which we haven't."

"A stolen load of cattle-feed, wasn't it? Somewhere in Lincolnshire, just after the war, when such things were devilish short?"

"Has that case been re-opened, then?"

"The stuff was for all of you—you two and his other brother?"

"Tom was still at school at the time."

"Just you two, then."

"Maurice and I had no idea where the stuff was coming from. We were paying Charles the market price for it."

"You're not exactly defending him, are you?"

"He didn't bother to defend himself."

"No. He pleaded guilty. We know. He got six months and took it quietly. Did you kill the fatted calf when he got home? The calf fattened with—"

Kenworthy was trying very hard to be insolent.

"It strikes me, Mr. Margerum, he must have been on to quite a good thing when he got home. He must have had things his own way for quite some time. I should imagine, seeing what he had saved you all. Is that how he got his hands on the deeds of Marsh Hall Farm? I can't help thinking that all in all he's quite a lucky man to have a parcel of land to his name."

"It's no business of yours what title he has to Marsh Hall Farm. If you need to know—which would surprise me—you can ask his solicitor."

"People who make me go the long way around usually have their reasons for it."

They were all by now thoroughly unhappy. Mrs. Margerum was tense. Old Margerum was not far from losing his temper. Kenworthy turned again to Maurice.

"Perhaps you'd like to tell us."

And Maurice took another of his sly looks at his father.

"As far as I'm concerned, I don't know why any of us are falling out over Charlie. I'm certainly not going to see myself incriminated by anything he's ever said or done."

"You do admit, then, that there could be some degree of incrimination? You're agreeing, after all, that what I'm asking is relevant?"

And this was too much for the father.

"We are admitting nothing of the kind. There is nothing to incriminate either my son or myself concerning a lorry-load of meal a quarter of a century ago. There is not—there cannot be, it is a fantastic thought—any connection between that incident and what happened to Miss Merridew. As for your suggestion that my step-son acquired his farm by means of—"

"Blackmail," Kenworthy supplied.

"The suggestion is nonsensical. And intolerably impertinent. Marsh Hall Farm belonged to his mother. She made it over to him by deed of gift when he came of age. That was three years before he went to prison."

"Thank you," Kenworthy said politely.

"And now perhaps you will concern yourself with your official business. You want, you say, to establish the reason for Miss Merridew's visit. I have been given to understand that it was concerned largely with the question of my granddaughter's schooling. If she came over here for a cup of coffee, it was for old time's sake—and not a very intimate old time at that.''

"Would you describe her as an inquisitive woman, Mr. Margerum?''

"I would describe her manners as impeccable.''

"But she was compassionate—interested in the troubles and sufferings of others?''

"You could say that. That is the vocation of a writer, I take it. Isn't that what lies behind all this digging up of forgotten ages?''

"Probably," Kenworthy said. "It could account for the special interest which she always evidently took in Charlie, don't you think?''

"It has always been a mystery to me why she took such an interest in him.''

"I'm sure it has. Now I'm going to ask you a very pointed question, Mr. Margerum. Do you think that your step-son murdered Cynthia Merridew?''

"You have no right to ask me that—and I have no way of knowing.''

"I think your tone implies that you would not be surprised.''

"Somebody murdered her.''

"And all this foul and silly business of rigging up an ancient lethal engine—doesn't it smack of the sort of talk that's been bringing her to Mawson's Drove for years?''

"She didn't get that sort of talk here, Mr. Kenworthy.''

"Over the road, then—''

"I've no idea what they found to talk about—over the road.''

"You know that from the books she wrote.''

Joe Margerum was even closer now to the picture that Wright had formed of him: unimaginative perhaps—but very loath to let go of an idea once he had formed one.

"I am not fond of Charles," he said at last. "You would hardly expect me to be. But I can't see him doing a thing like that—odd and irresponsible though he often is. Have you met him yet, Superintendent?''

"I shall do so presently.''

"I think you may decide that he could be capable of anything.''

It was Maurice's turn.

"You; what do you think?''

"You're asking me——"

"I hardly think you've forgotten the question. Do you think that Charles killed Cynthia Merridew?"

"It isn't a fair question. But I'll say no. I can't see him doing it. I can see him thinking about it. I can hear him talking about it. Doing it—no. He even hates wringing a chicken's neck."

"But he does when he has to?"

"Of course. He is a farmer."

"Do you like wringing chicken's necks. Mr. Margerum?"

Maurice looked astonished at the question.

"I never think about it," he said.

Kenworthy swung abruptly around to his wife.

"And what's your opinion?"

"Please don't ask me."

"Why not? Because you don't want to face up to a truthful answer?"

"Because you are putting words into our mouths."

"I'm not. I'm asking you to say what you think. Sergeant Wright, am I putting words into this lady's mouth?"

"You're asking her for her honest opinion, sir."

"Well—I'm not going to say anything."

"That's your prerogative," Kenworthy said, and then he suddenly adopted a lighter tone, as if he were some kind of entertainer who had dropped in to amuse them. "Now I'm going to ask you all another little question."

"For God's sake"—Joe Margerum was almost shouting— "stop playing games. Go out and get on with your work."

"Asking questions is my idea of work."

"Asking your kind of question is merely a gratuitous way of annoying honest folk."

"Annoying folk is sometimes the only way of finding out whether they are honest or not."

"I shall report the whole of this conversation to your Commissioner."

Kenworthy looked round the room with confidence. There was no doubt that he was enjoying himself. But Wright knew from previous experience that he was not wasting their time in the process.

"Listen carefully to the way I word it. And I want you to be equally deliberate in the way you answer. I want you to tell me what you think of the suggestion that Cynthia Merridew was murdered by Will Stratton.''

There was a hush—and then by way of anti-climax, Joe Margerum laughed.

"Mr. Kenworthy—it's you who ought to be earning your living writing stories—not Cynthia Merridew or my son-in-law—"

"From which I gather that your answer's no. You don't think it's very likely. You?"

He swung around to Maurice.

"Don't ask me. That was all long before my time."

"Do I infer that in one corner of your mind, you would admit the likelihood?''

"I think you're turning the whole thing into a fairy-tale.''

"Except that only a limited number of the characters lived happy ever after, Mrs. Margerum?"

"I have no connection with those days. They mean nothing to me. I have heard the name Will Stratton—"

"I'll bet you have."

"He's dead, isn't he?"

"Are you sure of that? Which of you is sure of that?"

Kenworthy looked into each pair of eyes in turn.

"We assume so," Mrs. Margerum said.

"Do you? How very convenient for you! And supposing I tell you that he is still alive?"

Old Margerum could stand this no longer.

"This is nonsense. Suppose he isn't dead? For my part, I neither know nor care. It's more than forty years since he took himself off. What connection could there possibly be between him and Miss Merridew?"

"Only that if he has been found, it might have been Miss Merridew who did the finding."

"And what would she want to do that for? And why bring him out to Norfolk? No one in this village would want anything to do with him."

"You don't think so?"

Kenworthy allowed himself a sad little smile.

"Don't you think that Charlie might?" he said. "His own father?"

And at that moment, Mrs. Margerum, whose cheeks had

been growing visibly hotter, finally let her emotions take control.

"Good God! You're not suggesting that Will Stratton is hidden away on Marsh Hall Farm?"

"I'd leave the door on the chain tonight, if I were you," Kenworthy said, "and get one of the men to answer it—preferably both of them—if anybody knocks."

·4·

"WHAT WAS ALL that about, Shiner?"

They were driving around the lanes—three miles of ruts and puddles—to cover the six hundred yards between Candle Mere Farm and the youngest brother's holding. The alternatives had clearly been either to get lost in the mist, or take one of the Margerums as a pilot.

Kenworthy switched on the wipers, and both men peered closely through the windscreen; but they were driving into an opaque wall. The mist was thickening.

"Stage-managed in advance," Wright said. "Till you messed them up by taking them through the wrong script."

"And stage-managed by whom?"

"The old man."

"In theory."

"Yes, I see what you mean, sir. The old man's been very much the boss there all his life. But Maurice hasn't got his father's nerve—he'd be inclined to be a bit more open with us, given the chance. And his wife would certainly give way altogether under pressure. They're all hiding something."

"How right you are, Shiner. The trouble is, it might not have anything to do with the case we're supposed to be working on."

"You don't think it's that load of pig-meal?"

Kenworthy made derisive noises in his throat and wound down his window to strain his eyes out into the mist.

"I said most of that just to get them rattled. A rattled man is apt to come out with a few home-truths."

"I suppose that's why you pushed Will Stratton at them, too."

Kenworthy suddenly stamped on his brake and reversed a

foot to release the end of the front bumper from the soft earth of the bank.

"We've no idea how old Will Stratton might be, Shiner. Could be seventy-five. What was the retiring age for public hangmen? Do you remember?"

"All right, sir. I'll concede that a man of Stratton's age might be physically capable of doing the job. But so might twelve million other Englishmen. We haven't heard the breath of a suggestion that Stratton is still alive."

"We have."

"From whom?"

"From me. Hang out your side, will you, Shiner? Look for a gate. Must be one here. I've been measuring out the tenths on the meter."

Then Wright had to climb out to attend to the gate-fastening, and the mud sucked down over the edges of his shoes. He was spattered from head to foot with filth and cow-muck when Kenworthy had to slip the clutch and spin his wheels to get going again.

"Take it from me, Shiner, Will Stratton is on the cards."

"It's also on the cards that Jack the Ripper has returned. Or perhaps Cornelius Vermuyden himself."

"Shiner, Shiner, Shiner—what has become of your pristine eagerness?"

"I can only say what I think."

"And you go on and say it, boy. That's what the taxpayer keeps sergeants for—to act as a brake on old men weary with experience. Christ! Not another bloody gate! Watch where you put your feet this time, boy—the car's beginning to stink."

Then they were pulling into a yard—horses, disturbed, stamping about in their stables, calves complaining, an overwhelming smell of ammonia from a sodden manure-heap. A light was switched on over a door—a dim incandescence, behind a halo, invisible if they took a couple of steps backwards.

"Getting worse."

Tom Margerum was the youngest of the family by something like ten years. Though he was by now in his thirties, he had still not lost the slenderness of his late adolescence. And with his vivacity, there went a certain racy candor. He looked more like a young commercial executive than a farmer.

"Come on in, then. And I know in advance: there are two corny questions you are going to ask me."

Kenworthy laughed.

"They've been on the phone, have they?"

"What do you think? I'm sorry, though, if they've buggered up your chances."

"More likely they've buggered up yours."

"How do you make that out?"

"Nothing worse than trying to work from an imperfect brief. Your father and your brother know about a quarter of the story. I know nearly half."

Tom Margerum grinned.

"You're honest, anyway."

"We do our best."

They were led into a room that contrasted violently with the other two that Wright had seen this evening: a dark paper with vertical stripes on two of the walls, a passable imitation of Westmorland slate over what had once been a fire-place—there were now four night storage heaters round the walls. In one corner was a Scandinavian desk unit in polished pine: a metal-tagged flop-over system of filing cards, trade leaflets for veterinary antibiotics. A dining annex, on a different level, had been cordoned off by a fence of wrought-iron scrolls, over which pot plant greenery entwined from a slatted rack of split cane.

Pride of place among the photographs was held by Margerum's wife, show jumping. There were also copies of the two pictures that Wright had seen at the Tennants'.

Sally Margerum had a youthfulness that made even Wright feel his own age: she could have passed herself off as eighteen, but she had the confidence of twenty-five—long hair, about her shoulders, a tee-shirt under which she did not seem to be wearing a bra, bell-bottom trousers with an immaculate crease.

"Do you want me to stay?"

"Please."

Her accent was Home Counties. She tossed her hair out of her eyes and looked penetratingly at each of them in turn. Her husband came to the point immediately.

"Point number one, Superintendent—I don't think my half-brother killed Cynthia Merridew."

"Good!"

"He's a rum bugger, is our Charlie—but I'll draw the line. And as for Comrade Stratton—I came on the scene well after even the tail-end of that business. I think there was still some ill-feeling when Maurice and Kate were kids. But to all intents and purposes I don't belong to the same generation."

"Quite."

"And having got that off my chest, may I offer you a drink?"

"I'd been hoping that you might."

There was a selection standing on a reproduction Jacobean dresser: Drambuie, Campari, Smirnoff, Pernod, Jameson's and Maclivet of Maclivet.

"Or there's a drop of home-brewed beer. Sally's been having a go with one of these kits."

"I'll settle for a pint," Kenworthy said. "And then let's take second things first, shall we? Charlie, Maurice and Kate. It must have been a strange household, when they were kids."

"I wasn't there."

"Don't keep reminding me. Your alibi is irrefutable. But you've heard them talk."

"It can't have been easy for any of them. Charlie always was one off. He was also, as it were, the sitting tenant. He was a few years older than the other two at the age when that gap mattered. My mother doted on him. And it's undoubtedly true that my father was always a bit hard on him. I'm not saying he was unkind: Dad hasn't got that in him. But when it came to putting Charlie on the farm, they were such poles apart—"

"You don't run these three places on co-operative lines, then?"

And Tom unloosed a guffaw in which his wife joined.

"Co-operative? Mr. Kenworthy, in these three farms, you've pretty well got a history of agriculture since the days when Adam delved and Eve span. Old Charlie—well, he's doing a sort of one-man Anglo-Saxon strip-system on that swamp of his. Oh, he'll accept iron plough-shares, you know, and last time he went to Lynn, he brought a drum of Derris back with him. But he's not a farmer, isn't Charlie—more like a bloody botanist. Dad—well, you can tell him anything in time. He can tell me a thing or two, over the rails at a market. If I was a sick pig, I'd as soon he sat up all night with me as any man I know. But try to talk marginal returns to him, or why it's bad economics to grow your own stock-feed on ground you could get under sugar-beet, and he thinks you're being disloyal to the soil. And if either of them wanted a new tractor, they'd ask me to buy it for them.''

"And your brother Maurice?"

"Maurice knows a lot—but the thinking has to seem to come from Dad, if you see what I mean. The deeds are in Maurice's name, now—but there'll not be much change while Dad's still alive. And Maurice might be past anything new by then."

The beer was deceptively strong and wholesomely bitter.

"So there is at least some degree of friendship between the three of you?"

"Let's be honest about it. Somebody else will tell you, if I don't. Charlie and I get on all right—largely by making sure that we don't have to get on too often. Charlie and the old man don't have anything to do with each other."

Kenworthy went back persistently to his earlier point.

"And when they were kids?"

"The younger ones hated Charlie. He bullied them—until they were old enough to bully him. But he had my mother's ear—and that went a long way. Until my father would suddenly get to hear of something, and come down heavily on the other side of the fence. Then there'd be a hell of a family row."

"For example?"

"I can't quote examples. I wasn't there."

"But you've drawn your own conclusions?"

"I thought it was Cynthia Merridew you were here to talk about?"

"She and Charlie were friends, weren't they?"

"Birds of a feather."

"What feather?"

"They shared a taste for cod's wallop."

"Was he bedding her?" Kenworthy asked, unexpectedly.

"What—an old girl of eighty-three?"

"She wasn't always eighty-three."

"What—Cynthia Merridew and our Charlie?"

It was plain that the thought had never occurred to him.

"My book is full of strange bed-fellows," Kenworthy said.

"So's mine, but—well, I'm buggered if I know."

"What was your own relationship with Miss Merridew?"

"Me? Pat on the head, quick look at the book I was reading, and a tanner for a bar of chocolate."

"So let's talk about Will Stratton, shall we?"

Tom Margerum offered beer again, but did not take any more himself.

"Will Stratton was just a name to me—one that they took good care I didn't hear too much of."

"That's what I'd have expected."

"What could I possibly know about him, Mr. Kenworthy?"

"People's attitude to him, that's all."

Tom Margerum paused for thought. He seemed to want to give a responsible answer.

"If you think he was the sort of figure who haunted my childhood, you are quite wrong. It may have been different in the case of the other two. There'd been Hitler's war in between, and that did a lot to make people forget things. It took the edge off, didn't it? Oddly enough, I don't think I did hear Will Stratton's name until I was twelve or thirteen—and then it was from my mother's lips."

Wright glanced involuntarily at the family group, in which Tom looked as if he had just come in from school.

"I'd been laughing at Charlie behind his back. He'd moved over to Marsh Hall by now, and we didn't see much of him. He came over, oh, I suppose nearly every day, and had a cup of tea with Mum in the kitchen. But he kept out of Dad's way. And even at that age, I could see that Charlie wasn't cut out for farming. He was talking about crossbreeding from Marakul rams, just because he liked the look of them. Anyone could have told me he couldn't feed them on the fen. But that's Charlie all over. My mother took me on one side and told me not to poke fun at him. There was more in Charlie than met the eye. Then she told me that my Dad was not Charlie's father. She said I ought to know before I was told by somebody outside the family. She mentioned Will Stratton's name, when I asked, that was all. She didn't look at me when she said it—and I never brought it up again. Obviously."

"What sort of woman was your mother?"

The question was put neither sentimentally nor casually. It was matter-of-fact, and yet at the same time there was the built-in suggestion that Kenworthy was personally interested. And Tom Margerum was mature enough to take it objectively.

"She was—I suppose you'd say she was a poet."

"And what precisely do you mean by that?"

And here Tom Margerum was stuck. The phrase had come impulsively. He was not articulate about matters of the mind. His wife came to his rescue.

"I know what Tom means—and it isn't that she used to write poetry. Though she probably did—"

"She did, as a matter of fact, when she was younger. But she would never show it to us."

"What Tom's trying to say, Superintendent, is that she was a woman who could get her satisfaction out of words and thoughts. I'm not saying she wasn't practical. She was a farmer's wife, and you'd only to look at Candle Mere Farm the way it was when I first saw it, to know that she was doing her job. But I didn't know her well. I only met her three times, and she wasn't at her best."

"Let's face it, Superintendent, she'd had, what do you call it, a traumatic experience. Will Stratton was that. She'd been protected. She was cultured—certainly by local standards, she was. She lived well. She was simple-minded in the best sense. She had no problems that she knew about. Then suddenly she was orphaned. And then seduced. I don't know how Will Stratton set about it. It's quite out of character, from all the accounts I've heard of him—and from what I know about her. But no doubt he could turn on a certain rough charm when he wanted to. A sort of gypsy-like character, that's the picture I've got. Soft burr in his speech; quaint turn of expression. Illusion of manliness, if that means anything—perhaps something more than just an illusion. Then he abandons her. Leaves her not only socially an outcast, but also with a reputation of having taken leave of her common sense. During that period when my father was courting her at a distance, she was desperately ill. For two years, she was barely conscious."

"And when she came to terms with it," Sally said, "it was on a plane of images and ideas that she kept very closely to herself. The other things—having babies, washing nappies, churning butter, and slopping about in the yard in boots with buckets—they helped, too, but in a different way. She had a certain mental self-sufficiency—a refuge that was hers and only hers. That's what I mean by being a poet."

"But why this sudden certainty that it all turns on Will Stratton?"

"I'll come back at you there," Kenworthy said, "and ask why everybody thinks it's so unlikely."

"Because I don't see the connection between Will Stratton and Miss Merridew."

"Oh, come, Mr. Margerum. We all know that she was interested in a human story."

"If you mean that she was a bloody busy-body, I'll go along with you."

"She also liked to follow things to their conclusion."

"You mean, she'd dug out Will Stratton?"

"I see nothing so very improbable in that."

And this made Tom Margerum think.

"The interfering bitch," he said at last. "And you think that Stratton may have been up here—lagered up with Charlie, perhaps?"

Kenworthy did not answer, but sat gazing at him, his blue eyes challenging him to think otherwise. At last Tom spoke.

"What would Charlie get out of it?"

"I don't know."

"I can see that Charlie would be keen to meet his own father. Anything to do with past history is a dead cert with him. Chuck is a bit of mystery and a personal relationship, and Charlie's hooked. But who killed Cynthia Merridew, and why?"

Kenworthy smiled benignly, and Sally Margerum laughed gently, seeing the funny side of the question.

"Now you know why we're here," Kenworthy said. "So let's come down to a more mundane level. Let's talk about Charlie's prison sentence."

"Not involved, Superintendent. Still at school."

"Even a schoolboy has certain things over the odds, that have to be paid for."

"Come off it, Kenworthy!"

"I'm serious."

"I knew nothing at all about it. Oh, I knew that something was on. They all stopped talking when I came into the room. Sent me out again, on some excuse or other."

"Were they worried?"

"Of course they were worried."

"In what sense were they worried? I don't just mean excited.

Were they frightened? Or tickled pink that Charlie was going to get his?''

"How would you expect me to know?''

"I've got an idea that you know very well. You're no fool, Margerum, and you were no fool as a boy. There are three possibilities about that load of meal. It might have been Charlie's personal fiddle—but that hardly consorts with the image of a dreamer with one foot in the Domesday Book and the other in the fen.''

"You haven't met Charlie yet, have you?''

"Or perhaps he was a tool in the hands of your father and your brother.''

"That shows how little you know of my father and my brother.''

"Or perhaps they were less interested in that meal than they were in seeing Charlie put away.''

"That's an outrageous bloody suggestion, Kenworthy.''

And Sally was beginning to look disturbed as she saw him lose his cool.

"You could help me to disprove it,'' Kenworthy said.

"How?''

"You could remember something.''

"What?''

"Anything you overheard.''

"I overheard nothing that made sense. There was nothing even faintly suggestive of a conspiracy.''

"Thank you. And what was the atmosphere like when Charlie came home?''

"I don't remember anything special about it.''

"No sort of party supper, or anything?''

"Not that I remember.''

"Was Charlie made welcome in your father's house? Or did you start seeing less of him than ever?''

"Roughly speaking, I'd say there was no change.''

Tom Margerum was rather calmer now.

"What was your mother's attitude, when Charlie went away—and when he came back again?''

"My mother—''

"Yes?''

"There was nothing devious about her. I presume that she

simply thought he'd committed a simple crime, tripped up and taken his punishment for it.''

"But you don't believe that, do you?"

"I'm not in a position to believe anything."

Then Sally intervened.

"Why don't you tell the man? It's all over and done with."

Tom Margerum did not look angrily at her but he did sit looking at her for several seconds with no kind of expression at all. He could even have been grateful to her for making the decision for him.

"I'm absolutely certain that Charlie wasn't framed. Dad and Maurice never ran to that kind of thinking. But—"

"But?"

"I think the three of them were in it together. And I think the other two were grateful to Charlie for keeping his mouth shut."

"It wasn't really dishonest," Sally said. "Nothing seems really immoral when you don't think there's a chance of your being found out."

"There was a lot of petty graft at the end of the war, and just after. But I don't know why you're resurrecting this."

"I'm not. I just wanted to know, that's all."

"I never said a word."

"Of course not."

Kenworthy stood up to go. Again the lamp over the door was switched on. It threw a diffuse light from which the corner of a shed stood out towards them. The boot of Kenworthy's car looked both familiar and strange—as if it had come from a world they had forgotten, and had no place here. For a moment it seemed that the mist had thinned while they had been talking. But they had not driven far before it was obvious that visibility was still as bad, if not worse. It was not one of those mists that hang in lambent layers, shifting occasionally to reveal a tuft of grass, a gate-post or the line of a rail fence. This was a solid wall of seemingly motionless drizzle, suspended between sky and earth, not really falling, but settling over everything, bonnet and windscreen, faces and the backs of hands.

At the first of the gates, Wright was startled by a rustle in the hedge behind him. A dog snarled, then barked angrily, then began trying to struggle through the undergrowth. For a second,

Wright was immobilized by fear. There was no doubting the savagery of the animal. It could have its teeth in his groin before he even saw it.

Then there was a thin whistle in the next field, repeated. At first the dog did not heed the call. Then a man's voice shouted.

There was a snuffle, a breaking of twigs. He heard the dog bound away into the night.

Kenworthy was indifferent.

"What's the matter, Shiner? Shucky dog?"

"No. Flesh, bone and teeth, this one. Mostly teeth. It was gnashing them."

"That's the way legends start. Probably half the folk-lore of this country started with imaginative young coppers."

"Why should a man be walking about in a field on a night like this."

"Watering his mangolds, probably. You're in the country now, Shiner."

"Somebody from the other farm, I'll bet. Council of war—"

"Let's bloody well hope so. If we haven't put the cat in this pigeon-loft, I've been wasting my breath."

·5·

"Time, Shiner?"

"Ten."

"Charlie won't be in bed yet. If he is, we'll pull him out."

"It occurs to me, sir—I haven't done the time-chart yet—when she arrived, when she was unaccounted for—"

This was Wright's chore at the outset of all their cases. He could not remember ever having producing a draft with which Kenworthy agreed.

"Leave it, Shiner. I've got it in my head. I expect they'll do one at the Center. And they won't try to pull things to fit our theories."

This time, Kenworthy parked the car while they were still a fair way from their objective.

"We make this approach on foot. It might be interesting to take this chap by surprise. And there are one or two things that might be worth a butcher's."

And now they really were certain that they could hear the sea. Charlie Margerum's territory ran down from the road opposite Candle Mere Farm to the waste strip that skirted the last reach of the estuary and the line of open sea: indeterminate pools and channels, reed-beds and desolation, haunted only by wild-fowlers, whose life might depend on the temperaments and whimsicalities of tides. Kenworthy and Wright stood for a moment and the mist ran down their eye-lids, congested their nostrils. Somewhere behind the stillness there was a very distant, very faint, very elusive roar. It was hard to be certain about it, because it never stopped; there were no waves in it, no breakers, no surf and no shingle. It was just a long, unplaceable, unchanging surge.

"Was it a night like this they let Luyk float? Do you think

he could see the water in the channel, or could he only judge the state of the tide from the sound of it? I wonder if he was sea-sick?''

Before they had walked far, they found that there were other good reasons, as well as a stealthy approach, for having left the car. Charlie Margerum's land was in no state to encourage visitors. The immediate surrounds of the house and yard were a slithering morass, and quite apart from seasonal difficulties, there must be something radically amiss with the land drainage. And there were other signs of manifold neglect: a gate on one broken hinge, which it was impossible to close again behind them. The door of a shed was open and banging against the wall. Broken windows in the house itself had been repaired with the sides of cardboard cartons.

Kenworthy was tempted by the outbuildings: a door here, a shed there, a miscellany of junk in a corner. But the premises rambled; it would have to be a job for a co-ordinated team. It could take a dozen men a day to search the place properly.

But suddenly Kenworthy stopped, stabbed the mist with his torch, and pulled Wright aside to look at a timber-pile.

''You never know your luck. This would take a bit of hiding, anyway.''

It was mostly a heap of sawn logs, but there were massive beams, too, perhaps relics of barn roofing. At the back, leaning against the wall, and shoring up the whole pile, were a number of huge quadrants, clearly once part of some composite structure, a sort of floor, sloping inwards to the center. The planking had been cut on the diagonal and reinforced by stout struts.

''Know what this is, Shiner?''

''I know it's what the scaffold was made from.''

''And do you know what it was before the scaffold was thought of?''

''It looks like something from a fairground.''

''How right you nearly are, Shiner. But it's rather a long time since you'd have seen one of those at a fair.''

''What is it, sir?''

''Let's go and ask Charlie.''

There was a front door, but when Kenworthy pulled the bell-handle, the frayed and rusty wire snapped. He hammered on the panels, but nothing was aroused beyond echoes suggestive of stone-flagged corridors. There was a window on either side of the door, neither of them curtained. They could see that one of the rooms was unfurnished. The wall-paper was damp-stained and peeling.

"We'll try the tradesmen's entrance," Kenworthy said.

And by then, if Charlie Margerum had leaned out of an upstairs window in a woolen night-cap with a blunderbuss levelled at them, they would not have been surprised. But the man who eventually came to the cheap stained glass panels of the back door was neither grotesque nor even unusual. He was wearing the trousers of what had once been a suit, threadbare, but not unclean. The upper part of his body stooped in a loose sea-man's jersey. His hair was curly and untidy—long, but not in the contemporary fashion. He looked as if he had a short back and sides every six or seven weeks—and was overdue for the next.

His eyes were alive without being shifty, moving from one man's face to the other, impelled by a lively curiosity and an attempt to see past surfaces into depth. His features were coarse—weathered, twenty-four hours behind a shave; grimy, but not gross. And when he spoke, his voice was slow—as if he did not talk often, and preferred to measure what he said.

"Good evening, gentlemen. Come in. I can't say your visit come as a surprise—"

He used the defective verb-forms of the East Anglian lands-man.

"You'll have to excuse the state of the house. That's the wrong time of the year for entertaining. That old mud get everywhere."

They followed him down a passage carpeted with old sack-ing. The treads of what had once been a servants' stair-case were bare, and had not been swept for years. Old articles of furniture—a wash-stand with a marble top, a walnut davenport, a discarded umbrella-stand—had been pushed up against a wall.

But the room into which he took them—and in which he clearly spent most of his time when indoors—presented a very different picture. It was large; it was over-full of possessions, it was organically untidy—but it was warm, thanks to a coal fire in a fire-place after the fashion of Adam—and it was clean. The grate and the trivet, on which a copper kettle was standing, had recently been black-leaded. A First World War shell-case, used as a stand for fire-irons, had been furbished up to a high polish.

Two walls were lined with bookshelves from skirting-board to ceiling: poetry—Byron, Hood, Longfellow and the Georgians; history—*Blomefield's Norfolk*, bound proceedings of county archaeological societies; standard collections of the Russian novelists in engine-tooled club bindings. Old copies of conservationist magazines were scattered about the table and chairs—a leaflet from Amnesty International. And Charlie Margerum took the *Financial Times*.

"Nasty night, gentlemen."

Kenworthy rubbed his hands in front of the fire, signalling to Wright that he was going to take his time, give Charlie Margerum his head. They had the whole night in front of them if they needed it. Wright knew at once that Kenworthy was going to like Charlie. This case was not going to be over by midnight. It was going to be expansive and leisurely—even if Charlie was the one they finally pulled in.

"Not a night for promenading on the Marsh," Charlie said.

"No."

"Sort of night you never know who or what you might run into."

"Ah."

"Sort of night for Long Amos."

"Not with you."

"That was a long time ago. Afore the Dutchmen came. You look at the old maps, before they dug the new levels, you won't find a coast-line like there is today. Time was when Ely really did stand on an island. When King John lost his wagon-train, trying to get over from Walsoken to Gedney, there really was a patch of water that he could get across at low tide. So in those days, that really did matter what sort of a sea-wall there was to keep the North Sea off. Well, that matter now. The way they leave that to Rural District Councils and the like, that only want a spiteful wind back of a bad-tempered tide, and we're back to where we were in 1953."

"Long Amos," Kenworthy reminded him.

"Yes, well, that was in the fourteenth century. Out Tydd Gote way. Lot of little old hamlets there—like a lot of small-holdings, each standing on its own fen. And all the able-bodied men used to take it in turns to ride out and watch the tide, whenever wind and weather looked like running the wrong way. Then if the bank was breached, they rang the bells at Tydd St. Mary and Walpole Island, and every man, woman and child who could swing a long-handled shovel—was swinging a long-handled shovel. Now Long Amos, he was duty-bound one night when a north-easterly was piling up the Lammas tides—only he was more interested in courting a young widow, out toward Sutton Corner—and he missed high water. And he missed seeing where the defenses had started to crumble, out past what's now the North Level. And of course there was two score drowned. And those that did manage to get inland, their land was ruined for well nigh two summers.

"But they reckon you can still run into Long Amos, back of the Roman Banks, when wind and water are in a bad combination. On a horse, only you never can see it, only hear it snorting and blowing. He wasn't there when he'd ought to have been, see—but he's been there ever since."

It was not a good story, and his telling of it was perfunctory. Why should a man, of dubious antecedents, visited as a crucial witness, under circumstances which he must surely know made him a primary suspect, open the proceedings by telling an irrelevant tale that was unimpressive and probably not even authentic? Because he thought it was expected of him? Because he wanted to create a fallacious impression of his mental state? Had Charlie Margerum enough brute shrewdness to cultivate his own eccentricities?

Kenworthy picked up the book that was lying open, face downwards, over the arm of Charlie's chair: Sweet and Myers on *The Survival of Minorities*.

"You believe in self-punishment when it comes to light reading, Charlie."

"I look on it this way. There are great minds in the world, and the least we can do is try to keep ourselves informed on what they are thinking."

Kenworthy read a paragraph, silently mouthing the words as he did so.

"Do you really go for this stuff? Do you really think that a relativist attitude to history can stop a race that's hell-bent on self-destruction?"

"I think there's a fundamental need for reassessment."

"But what does fundamental mean, in a relativist interpretation, Charlie?"

"Ah, now there you're a better-read man than me, Mr. Kenworthy. That's why I try to keep up with these things. I've got to admit that's sometimes heavy going."

Like many self-taught men with a taste for bookishness for its own sake, he had a strong taste for matter that was beyond him. It gave him an assurance that he was making progress.

"I'm afraid we've come to talk of other things," Kenworthy said.

"Yes, well—I can see that has to be."

Charlie waited for Kenworthy to show the way.

"This must have come as a shock to you, Charlie."

Charlie laughed—not humorously, not even nervously; he was chuckling over some private attitude.

"That's a good job you're not a suspicious man, Mr. Kenworthy."

"That's very fortunate for a lot of people."

"I mean—there's this poor lady, and what happened to her. And I wish I could get my hands on him that did it, that I do! And all carried out on a scaffold that I made with my own hands, and kept stored in my own yard."

Was the man utterly without guile? Or was he suffused with it?

"When was this, Charlie? When did you make it?"

"Five or six years ago."

"Why?"

"Miss Merridew—she asked me to."

"And you had to break up your cock-pit for the making of it?"

"You've got a sharp eye, Mr. Kenworthy."

"Miss Merridew used to come to the mains, too? She had a taste for fighting cocks?"

Charlie Margerum felt the weight of the kettle and eased it back on the trivet.

"Mr. Kenworthy—I reckon we've all of us, some time or other, done something that we wouldn't do again. Cock fighting now—that's an old English sport. That's how I used to look on it. Like the rat-pit, and fighting with the quarter-staff."

"I've seen the effect that a cock-fight can have on a woman.

Let's leave that for a moment. Why did Miss Merridew want you to make her a Dutchman's drop?''

''Shall I make a cup of tea, Mr. Kenworthy? Or we can have coffee, but it's only powdered stuff. Or I've all manner of home-made wine: elderberry, dead-nettle, parsnip, clover—''

''Presently, Charlie. Can we just concentrate for a few minutes? Why did Cynthia Merridew want a scaffold?''

''Well, you see, she was giving a lecture. To some of her friends. In London. And she wanted to make a film of it.''

''And did she make a film?''

Charlie nodded.

''Of the Dutchman's hanging?''

''Not the Dutchman. Herself.''

''In Mawson's Leam.''

''Not in the Leam, that was too public. In the old dike behind the paddock. She had to what she called transpose some shots of running water. She did that in the Leam.''

''And who took the film? You?''

''She showed me what I had to do—only I wasn't too good at holding that level.''

''Did you ever see the film?''

''She said she'd bring it and show me, but she never did.''

''Five or six years ago?''

''That's right.''

''And she came to see you at the beginning of this week?''

''That's right.''

''Why? What was she doing in Mawson's Drove?''

''There'd been some trouble at the school. She said that was one of her schools, and she wasn't going to have it upset.''

''What time did she come here?''

''Monday tea-time.''

''And how long did she stay?''

''Till about half past eight.''

''You must have been surprised to see her.''

''That I was! That I was!''

The man's vigor was almost puerile.

''So what did you talk about—for over four hours?''

''Old times. Old friends. Family matters.''

He used the term in a natural fashion. The Margerums might have been a close-knit group. But then, it was the only family group that Charlie had known.

"Can you tell us anything about Cynthia Merridew's relatives?"

"She never mentioned them—not in recent years, anyway. Years ago she used to. She'd come out with the name of somebody or other as if she expected me to know them. I don't think there's anybody left now—not in her own age-group, anyway."

"I see—Charlie—have you got a photograph of your father?"

And Charlie got up, opened a drawer in a cabinet and brought out a cheap album stuffed with snap-shots and post-cards. Only a few of them had actually been gummed in. He produced the unposed group with which Wright was already familiar.

"No. This wasn't the one I meant. Your own father, Charlie."

"You mean Will Stratton? Do you know, I don't think I ever did see a picture of him, Mr. Kenworthy. That's a funny thing. I don't think there ever was one in the family."

"Your mother never showed you one? She never talked to you about him?"

"She sometimes talked about him."

"Often?"

"Not often."

There was a dangerous temptation to talk to Charlie like a child. A certain child-like attitude, inherent in his temperament, had been reinforced by his isolation.

"What sort of things did she tell you about him, Charlie?"

"A lot of things—well, not a lot of things, really. Come to think about it, I don't suppose I heard her mention his name more than half a dozen times, all said and done."

"But those things she did say—they've stuck in your memory?"

"That they have."

"Such as?"

"How he came in on a neap-tide, and it was on a neap-tide that he went away again."

"And what did she mean by that?"

"A neap-tide, Mr. Kenworthy—that's the lowest that the flood ever run."

"So much I do know. But what did *she* mean by it? He didn't arrive here by boat, did he?"

"I never thought to ask. You know how that is, when you're a youngster. People say things to you—and you get a picture in your mind that nothing can ever shift. No; I don't think, now, that she meant he came by boat. I think she meant there was a neap-tide running the night he came."

"And a neap-tide running the night he left, I suppose?"

"That would be the color of it."

"Is that all she ever told you about the night he left?"

"She often thought about it."

"Thought aloud about it, you mean?"

"No. She didn't say her thoughts out loud. But I always knew what she was thinking. Leastways, I thought I did."

"And why do you think the tide meant so much to her? Did she take a great interest in the sea?"

"If you lived around these parts, Mr. Kenworthy, the rhythm of the water is your life."

Kenworthy treated himself to a sardonic smile.

"I can imagine that your mother was a little different from other women hereabouts."

"I know for sure she was, Mr. Kenworthy. And she loved it out here on the marshes. Often, she told me, she used to cut across the reed-beds of an evening on her stilts."

"On her *stilts*?"

"The old Fen Tigers' stilts, you know—they go back a couple of thousand years. The Romans, when they came, were scared out of their wits, because they thought there were giants hiding in the rushes."

"But a woman like your mother—"

"I'm talking about when she was a girl, Mr. Kenworthy, and a young woman. She never went about on stilts in my time. I never even saw a pair about the place—until I made my own."

Then Kenworthy suddenly changed the subject. It was one of his ways of keeping a subject talking without giving him time to think. In a preliminary bout, it was also a way of finding topics that might be worth exploring later in depth.

"I expect you have copies of all Miss Merridew's books?"

Charlie went to a book-case, and there was a collection of slim volumes together along one length of shelf. *Tales from the Marshes. More Tales from the Marshes. 'Twixt Welland,*

Nene and Ouse. He drew one out and handed it over. Petronius Arbiter: *Cena Trimalchionis*.

"Out of my depth here, Mr. Kenworthy."

"Out of mine, too."

Kenworthy looked briefly at the volume, not forgetting the dedication.

"I'll tell you what, Charlie—if this had been written today, in English, it would be on sale in Soho."

"She said that was strong meat."

"As far as I can see, that goes for a lot of her academic work. I'm no classical scholar—but I've heard of some of her favorite authors."

"She said if I found someone to translate them for me, I'd get a bit of a shock."

"Would it come as quite such a shock, Charlie?"

"How do you mean?"

Kenworthy was suddenly fixing him less than gently with his eyes.

"When you used to run the cock-pits, Charlie—"

"That was a long time ago, Mr. Kenworthy."

"How long?"

"Twenty, thirty years."

"People used to come from long distances, I would imagine."

"I was a younger man, Mr. Kenworthy—I was a bit wild. I didn't always stop to think things out."

"I'm not moralizing. I'm looking for facts. How often did you stage an event?"

"Twice a month. The second and fourth Saturdays."

"And then you stopped doing it."

"That's right."

"Just like that? Suddenly?"

"It all seemed wrong suddenly."

"Don't give me that, Charlie."

And Charlie was all at once confused, nervous—hurt.

"You aren't going to do me for cock-fighting, Mr. K.?"

"Just tell me why you stopped."

"I just told you—I began to see—"

"I'll tell you why you stopped, shall I, Charlie? You stopped when you saw what it did to Cynthia Merridew, didn't you?"

Now Charlie could no longer look them in the eye. And

Kenworthy suddenly started a dirty snigger. It took even Wright by surprise.

"I'll bet it fairly worked her up, didn't it, Charlie?"

"She got excited."

"I'll bet it was something you've never seen the likes of before or since. I'll bet you couldn't cope, could you, Charlie?"

"We're what you might call simple folk, in Mawson's Drove, Mr. Kenworthy."

"Did you give it to her, Charlie? Did you? I'll bet you did, eh? Or couldn't you, eh? How was it, Charlie? Bloody disgusting, wasn't it?"

"Mr. Kenworthy she was—she'd had a lonely life."

"So have you, haven't you, Charlie? Life's still pretty lonely, isn't it?"

Charlie looked at him with a sort of mute appeal. And Kenworthy achieved the apparently impossible. He unequivocally relented.

"Sorry, Charlie—I let myself get carried away sometimes. I'm bloody sure I couldn't have coped, either. And I reckon I'd have given up the mains."

"I broke up my pit, Mr. Kenworthy. As you know."

"And Miss Merridew stopped coming here quite so often?"

"She didn't come here for a long time after that."

"And did she ever refer to the incident again."

"It might never have happened. Mr. Kenworthy—I reckon you've got second sight."

"It does help, in my job."

And then an awful possibility seemed suddenly to dawn on Charlie.

"Mr. Kenworthy—you ain't a-thinking I had anything to do with the killing of her?"

Kenworthy couched his reply in tones of unassumed kindliness.

"Let's say that for your own sake, Charlie, we've got to talk it out. There are one or two little things I need to be sure about."

The last time Wright had heard him talk quite so sweetly, the man he was addressing had been under arrest within ten minutes. There was a moment of stillness in the over-furnished room. The books seemed to swell like surf on their shelves. The kettle began to sing, but no one paid attention to it.

"When Miss Merridew called here on Monday afternoon, was she alone?"

"She was on her own, yes."

"Where did she park her car?"

"She didn't bring her car. She came on foot from the village. Something was wrong with the car. She'd left it at Joe Procter's. The wheels wanted balancing."

This was true. The garage had reported it, and the fact had been on the file almost since the finding of the body.

"And she had no one with her?"

"I said—she was alone."

Charlie was irritated by the repetition of the question.

"She hadn't by any chance brought Will Stratton with her?"

"No—not this time."

Charlie's answer was as matter-of-fact as the question had been.

"Why do you say 'not this time'?"

"Because she'd promised to bring him one day."

"She knew where he was, then?"

"No. But she always said there was a way of finding out."

"How long had she been looking for him?"

"Off and on for years—of course, she had other things to do as well."

"Do you know whether she had made any progress?"

"She told me this last time, she was beginning to be hopeful. She'd come across some traces of him."

"Where?"

"Vale of Evesham way. She thought she'd found a grown-up son. My father was married, you know. To a girl he'd met on leave from the army. That was why he hadn't been able to marry my mother."

"Who told you that?"

"My mother."

There was something unreal in the dramatic simplicity of it. Kenworthy weighed it up for seconds before speaking again.

"Was Miss Merridew looking for your father while your mother was still alive?"

"She was, yes."

"And did your mother know that?"

"No. It was to be a secret."

"But if she'd found him—don't you think your mother might have wished she'd left well alone?"

"What was it that Miss Merridew always used to say? That there never are alternative levels of truth. There's only truth itself, and that's what she wanted to find out. And so did I."

"Charlie—did Miss Merridew, on Monday, say anything about the state of her inquiries?"

"She said she was beginning to be hopeful—because of something else she'd found out."

"And what was that?"

"She wouldn't tell me. But she did say that up to a month ago she'd been working on the wrong tack—looking in the wrong place."

"Not the Vale of Evesham?"

"It couldn't be, could it, if that's what she said?"

Something outside—it might have been the loose wire of an old wireless aerial—rattled against the window-pane. Charlie took no notice, and the other two sat quite still.

"Charlie—there's a question that I'm going to repeat. And I don't want you to be offended because I am asking it a second time."

Charlie waited, biddably.

"Charlie—when Cynthia Merridew called here on Monday afternoon, was she alone?"

"She was alone, Mr. Kenworthy."

"She hadn't brought Will Stratton with her?"

"No, Mr. Kenworthy."

"He isn't in this house at the moment—or anywhere about the premises?"

Was there any way of being sure of Charlie Margerum's depth and cleverness—or lack of it? Almost anything could be hidden under that almost caricature simplicity.

The wire caught the window again. Something—a mouse?— scurried along the passage outside. There was a scrabbling against a panel.

"No, Mr. Kenworthy."

The kettle spat boiling water over the bars. Charlie got up to it.

"It's time for that cuppa," Kenworthy said. "We'll join you in anything you normally drink at this time of night— except cocoa. It reminds me too much of army guard-rooms.

And while you're brewing up, we'd like to look through your photo-album.''

"I've got something better than that, Mr. Kenworthy.''

For a moment, they thought he meant a tipple. Then he came back from his drawer with a thick book, some five hundred pages of heavy quality paper, bound in full calf, and padlocked by a gold-plated hasp.

"My mother's diary, Mr. Kenworthy. I've never read it. That didn't seem right.''

"Have you the key?''

Charlie rummaged through the contents of another drawer: odd bits of sealing wax, broken watches, thimbles, a jew's harp. He could not find it.

Kenworthy brought out a pipe-cleaner and fiddled about for a few seconds. He opened the book and read an entry at random.

"My God!'' he said.

·6·

SOMETHING LIKE TWO thirds of the book had been filled. It fell naturally into three sections, and one of them—toward the end, but not including the last twenty or thirty pages—had been sealed off and wrapped round with three bands of surgical tape. Quite unnecessarily, it had been plastered to the page with blobs of red sealing wax.

The earliest entries were in an immature, school-girl's hand—not graceless, but rather cramped. Throughout her diary life, she had seemed to want to economize in paper.

The war is over, and even the gulls behind the plough seem to know we are at peace again. Went late this afternoon to the fowlers' shelter beyond the Leam. Saw a red-necked grebe, sure sign that winter is on us. Also thought I saw a Great Northern Diver, but probably mistaken. Too much zeal! Imagination not a good thing, in bird-watchers!

Lovely to stand on the surf-line, looking out to sea, and not fancy I can hear big guns on the other side. Not that I ever did, but the thought was never far away. Wonder how soon they'll start sending the soldiers home—men like Daddy, who have been out there since the beginning?

Then followed the years when motoring came the way of the Franklins.

We all had to get out while Frank filled up, because the petrol-tank is under the front seat. And the men got out and followed us on foot up Heacham Hill; the radiator was boiling over like a railway engine.

There were dances: Candle Mere Farm versions of a May Ball, with vast buffet suppers on the lawn—and the weather miraculously obliging.

> *Surprised that Daddy didn't object to the Charleston and the Shimmy. I am sure that before the war he would have been horrified. Mummy still is! Had to fob off the Renton boy. I know acne is not infectious, but I hate to sit studying it with quite such microscopic precision. I tried not to be unkind to him, but I am afraid I shall have to sooner or later.*

Her mother died:

> *Daddy bore up like a soldier—which he is!—at the grave-side. Uncle Robert (Gordon) pompous as usual. Aunt Tilda criticized the sandwiches, saying it was wasteful to cut the crusts off. Some people think of the most appropriate things!*
> *Most of all, I wanted to go out and put the reeds between myself and everybody—to stand where the brown water swirls around the glistening banks and finds its way home. But I can hardly leave Daddy tonight. Must content myself with sitting on the window-sill, listening to the night. I can hear Robin Peachey's oars, everything is so still.*

Then she was finding a sort of girlish pleasure in her command of the household.

> *Made syllabubs for supper-time. Not quite what they should be. Harriet says I should have used Madeira instead of sherry. Daddy didn't seem to notice. At first I thought he was just being polite—but he seems so far away so much of the time. He is so desperately unhappy, and I cannot think of anything to say or do to help him. I sometimes think he could get through a whole meal, these days, without knowing what he has had to eat.*

Kenworthy held the book on his knee so that Wright could look over. But they did not always finish a page at the same time—and Kenworthy was skipping some of the entries. Charlie produced a tray and cups from a cupboard at the side of the fire-place. He made the tea with his back to the two men, and paid no attention to their reactions.

Maud Franklin had a holiday in Bournemouth. She managed to persuade her father to come down for a few days, and he seemed to find something of his previous spirit, even though he had protested strenuously at being taken away from the farm.

I dare not let him know how I pity him. They adored each other, and they had been parted from each other for so long. And he had been home less than three years.

The Renton boy's attentions seemed to have evaporated. There was no mention of any final need to put him in his place. His name simply disappeared from the pages. Perhaps, in her new maturity as mistress of the house, she was beginning to appear hopelessly forbidding to a spotted male.

But maturity did not bring unqualified independence. She wistfully wrote on one page that she had been able to get further afield when she was fourteen than she could now she was twenty-two. But she did not explain the reasons for these relative restrictions. Perhaps it was because, as an unaccompanied female, she had begun to arouse embarrassing interest in any neighborhood where she was not immediately familiar. Her local excursions were mostly limited to the water-logged wilderness between the boundaries of Marsh Hall and the edge of the Wash. But she was loyal to this tract. Once, often twice every week—on the long light evenings of May and June, every day without fail between tea and supper—she was parking her bicycle against the culvert over Mawson's Leam, striding out among the clumps of marsh grass and sea lavender. She knew the nests of water-rail and spotted crake. She did not write of ever putting a gun to her shoulder, but she clearly knew the lore and language of duck-shooting, and referred often to the time of day passed with this or that fowler or naturalist— local figures undetachable from the marsh, they seemed always to be there, waiting, watching, ruminating. But mostly she was laconic about detail; almost always she came home to record some pantheistic impression of vastness and solitude, of teeming creation or primeval sterility. Sometimes there was an extravagant image.

A sunset that looked as if God had stirred up the mackerel sky with an eel-pilger.

"Where and what is Hickling's?" Kenworthy asked.

Charlie Margerum was emptying a packet of wholemeal biscuits into a tin with a conical lid.

"That's the fowler's hut, about three quarters of a mile over the Leam. There used to be a couple of punts moored in there. You could float out down the dike to the Old Drove Channel at high water."

"It seems to have been a favorite spot of your mother's."

"That was a favorite spot of mine, too, when I was a boy. I still go back there sometimes."

Maud had not made an entry every day. Indeed, one day she had written, excusing herself for a week's default, that if a diary became an obligation, it ceased to be a friend.

But there was, one night when she sat up late with pen in hand.

Ventured far round the shore at full flood of the neap tide. Stood and watched a ripple on the water like a quivering of cat's fur.

Pathetic fallacy! A sickle moon, rising gold rather than silver from a hundred pools and ditches. One of those nights in the prime of the year when, from twilight to dawn, it never grows wholly dark.

At half past ten, when she was crossing the old sea-wall at the point where it was pierced by the Leam, she felt she could still have seen to read. But as she came up the bank approaching the lane, she began to walk more hesitantly. A small group of men were arguing fiercely—and she had begun to be afraid of men.

Two of them were villagers known to her by sight and name—laborers, not dull-witted, but prejudiced, and with a horizon limited to the boundary sedge. The third was a young man whom she took at first to be a foreigner: swarthy in complexion, dark of hair and eye, slim and strong. He had asked them the way to somewhere, and they, belonging to the generation which perhaps had its reasons for distrusting strangers, had answered aggressively and ambiguously. Moreover, both sides were unfamiliar with each other's mode of speech, and were apt to construe the unusual as an attempt to be different and clever. The stranger, hot-blooded, had interpreted their bucolic prudence as animosity—as, indeed, it was—and the issue had reached a point where satisfaction was about to be sought in concrete terms.

As Maud Franklin brought her bicycle across the verge into the road, the two cottagers touched the peaks of their caps.

"Evening, Miss Franklin. Chap here been asking the road to Candle Mere Farm."

"Well, I'm sure he means no harm, George. And it *is* a public highway. I'm going home now. He can come along with me."

He stood looking at me with eyes that seemed hungry to search and find. The other two were uncertain whether they ought to entrust me to such company for the half mile that I had to walk.

"Reckon us ought to come along of you."

"That's all right, William—I know this man."

I don't know what possessed me to say such a thing. It was on the spur of the moment. I thought, a second later, that I must have taken leave of my senses.

After the first few yards, Will Stratton was pushing her cycle. He laid his old army kit-bag across the handlebars and saddle.

"You must be Miss Maud."

"That's right. How do you know my name?"

"I recognize you from your photo."

The speech of Norfolk is not without its music, but this man's was a different melody, the ullulating diphthongs and burred consonants of the West.

"I never thought—why, morning and night for nigh on four years, in tents and dug-outs, I used to look at that little picture. You were on one knee on a piano-stool, and you had your hair in a ribbon. And your mother—how is your dear mother?"

She told him the news.

"And the Captain? I trust he's well."

It was like—well, not like at all, really—something out of Treasure Island. *Old Pew arriving at the country inn.*

*And yet no resemblance to Old Pew at all, of course—
nothing like so sinister. But there was something deli-
ciously sinister about it, all the same: a phantom, and yet
he was not a phantom at all, a live man, marching like
a soldier and talking like a minstrel, who has stepped out
of a chapter in my father's life about which none of us
knows anything.*

Charlie Margerum passed round the tea. It was very strong,
richly brown, and he put three heaped spoons of sugar into his
own.

Old Franklin had been delighted to welcome his former servant—but there was a gravity in the way he questioned him—
and a clear implication that the things they had to talk about
were not for his daughter's ear. She made herself scarce about
the kitchen and prepared a plate of cold mutton and mustard
pickles for their visitor. Then she left them talking in the draw-
ing-room and went upstairs to her diary. Will slept that night
in the room that her father no longer used as a dressing-room,
but the next morning carried his kit-bag into the shed where
her father found him a bunk-house bed.

In the subsequent weeks there was little mention of him in
the pages, and when he appeared again, a couple of months
later, it was a bald reference such as might have been made to
any servant who had spent a life-time with the family.

*Talked to Will while he creosoted the new fence over
by Margerum's. I love the smell of warm tar and new
timber.*

Kenworthy turned over a handful of pages, then ran his
fingers along the inside of the spine of the book. A couple of
pages had been torn out.

"She's deprived us of one of the interesting bits," Wright
said quietly.

Kenworthy glanced at the entries on either side of the gap.

"Depends what you're interested in. That was what she
wrote—or tried to write—when her father died."

Only a few pages further on they came to the chapter that
had been sealed off. For the time being, Kenworthy left this
and went straight over to the closing pages, of which there

were not many, and which were separated from what had gone before by a number of blank sheets.

The handwriting now was markedly changed. After the characterless cursive hand with which the diary had opened, and the flowing, sometimes barely legible vigor of the early adult years, there was now a sort of uneasy care—a finickiness of curve, an uncertainty of loop, the beginnings of flourishes that did not end up as flourishes at all. This was the period immediately following her return from breakdown and convalescence.

People were kind, that was the phrase, and that was the spirit. It was also implicit that no one understood her, and that there was no one whom she could consider a friend: except young Mr. Margerum, who farmed on the other side of the fence that Will had creosoted. Clearly he was beginning to be assiduous in his attentions. And it was equally clear that they were not entirely distasteful to her—though she seemed to think that she had treated him badly at some unspecified point in the past. The time was soon reached—it took about six weeks—when the only entries were those concerned with Joe Margerum.

But before this, there was a joyful reunion with her infant, now approaching two years old. About a month after her homecoming, the family doctor had expressed the opinion that she was now perfectly fit to look after the child—he thought, in fact, that it would be positively good for her to do so.

There was a convincing—if embarrassing—paragraph about the weight of the baby on her shoulder. It was difficult to look at Charlie and feel that one was getting the right picture. He was now sitting quietly while Kenworthy and Wright were reading. The stubble about his jaws was uneven in both density and darkness. When he had shaved a couple of days ago, he had shaved badly. His knees, as he splayed them out in front of the fire, displayed their contour under his shapeless trousers.

His mother had been thrilled to have him back—but when it came to recording her feelings, she had lost much of her talent for evocation. There was no lyrical energy in the ensuing pages—only an attempt, dutiful towards herself—to find it. It usually petered out into an artificial nostalgia—even, in places, into a self-inflicted melancholy. Her walks abroad now were sedate and unadventurous: no more wandering on the marsh.

She was limited to the hedgerows of paddocks, occasionally trod the lanes, but never seemed to go beyond the parish boundaries.

That was as far as concerned her walks alone—or with Charlie in a push-chair. With Joe Margerum there were excursions further afield: Yarmouth and Lowestoft, shopping afternoons in Norwich, a motor-boat on Oulton Broad. There was scintillant pleasure in all this, but briefly stated, and never anything that had her writing by the midnight oil. Not, that is, until Joe Margerum proposed to her. It came hardly as a surprise, and she did not keep him waiting for an answer. But perhaps she wished she could have found it in her heart to do so.

> *I should have felt like someone in one of those wearisome novels if I had said, "I will tell you tomorrow—or this time next week." And what would I have said tomorrow or this time next week that could have been different from what I said tonight? He stood by the window, waiting for me to speak, and the devotion in his eyes was only matched by the suspense in his heart.*
>
> *How could one hurt such a dear, kind and selfless man? In any case, I would be a fool—*

That was almost the last entry. There were a few other outings. There was a long, prosaic statement of the practicalities of their settlement: Joe Margerum to move over to Candle Mere Farm and Drove Farm to be let to a bailiff on an agreed lease that would allow it to revert to the family as needed. The existing lease of Marsh Hall—to a man who farmed it more or less as an independent holding—was not to be interfered with during the active life-time of the tenant; but it was understood that, other essentials falling into place, it was ear-marked for Charlie.

"Would you rather have had Drove Hall than this place?" Kenworthy asked.

"I love this farm," Charlie said, and there was no doubting his sincerity.

"All the same. I'm no agriculturalist, but I can see that Drove Hall is the better farm. Better soil, better drainage, no waste—I mean, what *could* you hope to do with half the land you've got, short of a major engineering project? And this house is a white elephant—''

''It's all I ask.''

Kenworthy turned to the final pages. There were practical notes in preparation for the wedding. It was as if Maud had almost ceased keeping it as a diary, and were now merely using the book for personal planning. There was a perfunctory essay in self-assessment and dedication on the eve of the event: Maud counting her blessings, and perhaps trying to convince herself of them. There was no entry on her wedding-night; perhaps she had left the book at home. She never confided in it again.

''They say,'' Kenworthy said, ''that two kinds of people keep diaries—the very miserable and the very happy. The moral seems to be that Maud Franklin's marriage to Joe Margerum made her neither.''

Now he turned back to the sealed pages and pulled out his pen-knife.

''Charlie—I'm sorry about this. I'm afraid we're going to have to break into the secrets.''

''You know what's necessary, Mr. Kenworthy. For myself, those tapes were always my mother's message that she never wanted me to read what she'd written.''

''I think you're wrong there, Charlie.''

And Charlie looked keenly up without comprehension.

''The reason why your mother didn't ever destroy this book—one of the reasons, anyway—was so that you or I, or somebody like us, should one day peruse it and learn what we can. When she sealed off those particular pages, it was herself she wanted to prevent from ever reading them again.''

He slipped the blade of the knife between two pages, but the tape was tougher than he had expected, and he had to saw at it to part the strands. The ineffective blobs of sealing-wax cracked away from the paper. Then the pages fell naturally open where something had been placed between them.

It was a post-card, sepia tinted, which suited the uniform of the man that it portrayed.

''There you are, Charlie—that's your father.''

He handed it over with no more than a cursory glance, and Charlie studied it with an interest that was hardly short of wonderment. But when he judged that he had seen enough of it, Kenworthy stretched out his hand for it.

"You'll let me have it back?"

"Of course. I have to hang on to it, for obvious reasons. But I'll have a copy made for you as soon as we get back to the office."

The portrait was of a young man, slender, with a tanned complexion and intense black eyes. He was wearing the service dress of an infantry private—brass buttons, puttees, a tunic tight at the collar. It was a studio pose—he had been made to stand by a chair, with his feet planted squarely apart, and from his hand there dangled casually a thin swagger cane, with cap and ferrule of silvered metal. It had obviously been taken in the earliest months of the war—probably before Stratton was first sent to France—some years before Maud Franklin was to meet him.

Kenworthy laid the post-card on the table and turned his attention to the diary again. Then he looked up and listened—and the other two heard something, too. There was a distant banging, and the sound of it sent the mice in the passage scurrying for shelter.

"Charlie—there's somebody in the house."

For an instant, all three listened again: a hammering, and then a voice shouting. Charlie shook his head and got up, and Wright and Kenworthy followed him along a series of corridors, taking, after the first turn, a different route from the one by which he had brought them into the house. In monochrome reproductions hanging beside a tile-backed hallstand, the Victorian ideal of girlhood looked on with waxen-cheeked serenity. They were at the front door at which they had first knocked. A smell of must came from one of the rooms beside it, whose door was standing open.

The bolts needed strong handling. They had not been opened for a very long time, and the door was swollen in its frame.

Charlie hauled it open and two police constables in flat caps were standing there, their Ford Escort waiting on the pebbled drive.

"We were told you were here, sir. The Chief Inspector has sent us. Major Tennant has been to the Center. His little girl is very upset—and it seems she has something to tell you which he thinks you ought to know at once. The Chief Inspector, sir—he said we ought to tell you, anyway—"

It was all played out with prudence and protocol. Kenworthy went back for the diary. Charlie looked disappointed that they were leaving. It was a ticklish job reversing the car in the spot where Kenworthy had left it.

OVERNIGHT, SOMETHING SEEMED to have happened to the weather-map. Fronts had fled or faded. Vortices had spun and side-stepped; barometers reacted smartly to tapping fingers. When Wright and Kenworthy looked out in the morning, a ruthless north-easter was sweeping across fore-shore and marsh, dissipating the last of the mist—such of it as had not fallen as hoar-frost on grass blades and broken twigs, or on the roof of Kenworthy's car and the spiked iron chains round the forecourt of the *Red Lion*.

The schedule of Cynthia Merridew's known and probable movements had been drawn up—and pretty thin it turned out to be. A few minutes after nine—almost as soon as Heathcote had called his register, she had drawn up outside the school. There was casual evidence that she had driven into the village as if approaching from one of the London roads. She had stayed in the school until the mid-morning play-time. At ten thirty she had taken her car to the garage, and at ten thirty-five she had walked into the *Red Lion*, expressed disappointment that there had been a change of landlord since her last visit, had ordered a coffee, been to the lavatory, played hell because one of the hinges of the seat was broken, and had then sat in the saloon bar, writing furiously for three-quarters of an hour.

She had left the pub at noon, and had then met a bearded gentleman at the southern limits of the village in circumstances that suggested a firm appointment. This had been the tearful, hysterical and frustratingly vague evidence of Pamela Tennant, which had drawn Kenworthy and Wright away from their study of the diary in Charlie's living-room. And there were only three bearded men in Mawson's Drove. Pamela knew them all, and Miss Merridew's escort had not been one of them. She described him as an old man—but when, tested by way of comparison, she also thought that Wright was old, Kenworthy had to exercise exceptional self-control. Her description of the man's clothing was equally unhelpful. She thought that he was well dressed; but she thought that her Uncle Charlie was well dressed, too. The car was an Austin Cambridge, grey, F registration, not known at the Mawson's Drove garage. She had not taken in the remainder of the number plate.

The pair had driven out of the village southwards, the way Miss Merridew had come in. No one had seen her come back—but she could not have been away long, for she was calling at Candle Mere Farm—on foot—just after two. Inquiries were put in hand at all the accessible pubs at which they might have lunched, but so far they had yielded nothing.

From Candle Mere Farm she had gone across to Marsh Hall. It was conceivable, even probable, that walking in leisurely fashion, standing and staring as much as the mist made worth while, she went straight from the central Margerum's farm over to Charlie's.

According to Charlie, she had spent about four and a half hours with him. That could have left her with no time for anything except to make her way over to the Tennants. There was no suggestion that she had given any thought to finding accommodation for the night. The garage had assured her, on her acid insistence, that her car would be ready by half past three in the afternoon, and the implication seemed to be that she intended to leave the village that day.

There was no reported sighting of her after she left the Tennants. She had walked out of the bungalow into mist, but had staunchly refused the Major's offer to escort her as far as her car. She enjoyed, she said, solitude and meditation. After that, she was not seen alive again by anyone prepared to talk about it. No one spoke of seeing her on the Tuesday at all. The pathologist timed her murder—the first hanging—at between ten and midnight on the Tuesday night. The body had been found on Wednesday, at first light, by a fowler out, so he said, for foreshore duck—it was the close season for every other species.

"Shiner," Kenworthy said, "I'm not going to play this according to the book."

"No, sir."

This was alarming in itself. One did not associate Kenworthy with orthodoxy, but he usually innocently claimed to be keeping all the rules. Kenworthy announcing that he proposed to throw procedure to the winds was the herald of chaos.

"Come for a walk."

That was an excuse to get away from other policemen. They did not go far: along the street to within sight of the marsh.

"I'm going back to London, Shiner."

"Yes, sir."

"Don't look so down in the mouth. Have you still got it in for me for hogging the diary?"

"I don't see what else you could have done."

Last night, when they had finished with the Tennants—and it had been a wearisome shambles of an interview—there had been no more obvious destination than bed. Kenworthy and Wright were much closer operators than many of their colleagues, but they stopped short of sleeping together. It had been natural for the Old Man to take the book with him, and that was the last Wright had seen of it. It had not been mentioned at breakfast time.

"I'm going off to London. I doubt whether I shall be able to get back tonight."

So the crafty old bugger was working himself a night at home, was he?

"I'm leaving you here, and I see no reason why you should die of boredom. The Chief Inspector—"

Wright felt his blood pressure drop. The day's prospects suddenly became as appetizing as a plate of cold casserole. He had nothing against the Chief Inspector, but he was familiar with the form. Men had to work together without the time, chance or inclination to get to know each other. The decision to call in Scotland Yard was made at Chief Constable level. Less senior officers were apt to think they could have done the job as well themselves—and it was the unknown invading junior who came in for all the accumulated spleen. If anybody's time was going to be wasted today, then Wright's was—

"The Chief Inspector knows you're working for me. You've got a full day in front of you, and I've left him under no illusions about it."

"Thank God for that."

"I want you to go around the women—"

"Sounds promising—"

Kenworthy looked at him with cold contempt. There was only one man allowed to crack jokes before the day was properly in motion. Wright promptly regretted this ebullience. And there was no harm in saying so.

"Sorry, sir."

"Know what you're looking for?"

At least, he knew the answer to this. They had been over this ground before at other times in other places.

"No, sir."

"Good. Much more likely to learn something that way. I shall want to know it all. But stick to the women. The men are likely to be a team. Some of the women may possibly have an outlook of their own. Isolate them. Get them away from the men-folk by any way that suggests itself. Go back to the methods of your youth, if you like. Take Kate Tennant—"

Kate had set on the edge of the settee last night, waiting every minute for the fracas which, as it happened, had not broken out this time. There must be limits to her fun, living with a man who still fancied himself a Major. But perhaps she still thought she was a Major's wife—perhaps she missed the Regimental Quartermaster's wife, and the Adjutant's wife, and the Battalion Intelligence Officer's wife, to all of whom she had a superiority in protocol. It was difficult to imagine how far she had gone along with her husband in his last-ditch stand over the village school. How far had she been from revolt when she saw—as she must have seen—the effect it was having on the child?

Certainly, last night, Tennant had shown himself utterly obtuse as to what might be going on in the mind of the child. Pamela, who had earlier woken screaming in a nightmare, had been put back to bed, and they had succeeded in getting her off to sleep again. But Tennant—who had raged about the child's stupidity in not telling them earlier about the bearded man—had insisted on waking her and bringing her downstairs to answer questions personally. When she had not immediately remembered all the detail she had told her parents, he had started to bully her. The mother had intervened, and when a row developed between the pair of them, Kenworthy crudely ordered them out of the room—Wright, too—so that he could question the child in his own way.

"I let her see for a couple of minutes what it might be like to have a proper father."

But the information he had gleaned had been no more than had been recorded in the time-chart.

"Get that woman apart from her husband for half an hour, Shiner—and God knows what you might learn. Some of it might even possibly have something to do with the case. It would be criminal negligence to overlook the possibility. And just remember that Kate Tennant was a Margerum. If you can split her loyalties, that's the way she'll lean."

"Yes, sir."

"Then there's Heathcote's wife. Go and ask *her* why Miss Merridew signed herself Cynthia in her husband's book. It might be interesting to get a view on la Merridew from someone who had neither a professional nor a literary commitment."

They had to step on to the grass edge to allow a tractor to pass them. Maurice Margerum was at the wheel, a shapeless felt hat pulled down over his forehead. He was towing a trailer loaded with cattle fodder.

"I doubt whether that man's wife is going to help you much. Probably no more than the pudding she looks. Probably a daughter of the soil herself. But she was a worried woman when we were up there last night—and of course, that might be no more than the general strain of events. But it might also have been because there was one particular turn that she didn't want the conversation to take. Find out. Chat her up. Make love to her up against the scullery copper, if it helps. But get her talking. Any woman married to a Margerum must be leading an existence of her own on some plane or other, even if it's only an imaginary one. Then there's Tom's wife."

Wright retained a very vivid memory of the girl with the grave eyes, shaking the hair from her temples. It wasn't every day of the week that a run-of-the-mill detective-sergeant could insist on a tête-à-tête with the likes of Tom's wife.

"And I wouldn't try too much on with young Sally, if I were you. Knows how to snaffle a sixteen-hand stallion at a water-jump, that one does."

"All the same, most of what we learned from Tom was through her intervention."

"And she'll know where to draw the line. Even if you can't pull her over it, you might find out where it lies."

Kenworthy suspected more than he saying, but now was not the time to put questions that Wright was expected to answer for himself. Kenworthy never cared to explain things that he expected people to see. It was signposts that he was in a mood for supplying, this morning—not maps.

"So you ought to have enough on your hands to keep you out of the Chief Inspector's hair—"

"Yes, sir."

"Any time you have left over, you can spend with Charlie. You can go and keep Charlie Margerum company for as long as you like—once you've accounted for the women."

Kenworthy looked out over the marsh, then opened his brief-case for his field-glasses."

"Only not today you won't."

"Sir?"

Kenworthy passed him the binoculars, and Wright saw that a man was pulling at the oars of a dinghy in the lower reach of the Leam. Thigh-boots turned down at the knees, sou'wester jammed down over his ears, the same bosun's jersey he had been wearing last night; there was no mistaking Charlie Margerum.

"Oughtn't we—?"

"What—alert the coastguard or something? Where do you think he's going, Shiner? Holland? China? Probably fancies stewed eel for his supper. Maybe thinks a day's fishing will do him more good than digging land-drains, mending windows, or feeding starving bullocks. Perhaps he thinks he's an incarnation of Long Amos. Perhaps he just wants to think a few little things out—put himself out of reach of other Margerums for an hour or two."

"You're pretty sure that this turns on a conspiracy of Margerums, aren't you?"

"I wouldn't bet a month's salary on it. But I'm prepared to scuttle the ship for a long, cool look at Will Stratton."

Wright knew this. He knew that Kenworthy was committing himself to a conception that might come whanging back at both of them, if it proved a waste of time. It was not exactly like him. He was frequently impulsive—or took pains to appear theatrically so—but he was seldom incautious. This might be something intuitive. He often pretended that his solutions were; but in the final count they were generally founded on some astute reading between the lines that he had kept to himself for the satisfaction of startling his colleagues. The Yard was split between men who begrudged Kenworthy his dramatic instincts, and men who didn't. But Kenworthy did not care; he could always throw his record in the faces of his critics.

He looked at Wright now, read his mind and grinned.

"I'm going to a lot of trouble to keep you out of this, Shiner. You're too young, as yet, for brilliant failures. Oh, and I'm sorry—it's all in the book—"

Exaggerated apology; unnecessary pretense that it was all an oversight, when all the time he was inventing stage climaxes, just for his own amusement. He put his hand in his briefcase and brought out the diary.

"It's all in there, Shiner. Better read it before you pay any calls."

He looked at his watch.

"Train from King's Lynn. I must go and get him."

Him? Of course. Will Stratton.

"Of course, sir."

Kenworthy waved merrily.

"Of course," Wright repeated, for the sake of a pair of sea-gulls and a tall dry stalk of dead hog-weed. Then he opened the diary at the first of the pages that had been sealed.

Why does everybody think a woman is capable of nothing? Edward and Ray have done nothing but quarrel since my father died, and if I try to intervene, each blames the other for what he himself hasn't done. I told Ray we had winter moth in the Bramleys, which he vehemently denied, and when I finally got him to use the spray, he mixed it twice as strong as it says on the drum. You'd think the man can't read. And when I pointed that out to him, he looked at me as if I was saying I can mound potatoes as fast as he can. This afternoon Edward was supposed to be double-digging a new onion bed; but he was only tickling the surface. If it wasn't for Will, this place would come to a stand-still.

The wind blew spiteful in Wright's face and lifted a corner of the page. This was no place to be reading. A reed-bed heaved and bristled, as if it were trying to outdo the distant surf. Charlie

Margerum was temporarily out of sight. A skein of geese, not very many, ten or a dozen birds, flew in an imperfect and depleted V to no rational destination.

Wright tucked the book under his arm and walked back to the village.

·8·

THERE WAS NOWHERE for him to go but an office corner of the headquarter compound. But Wright did not get as far as that. He saw Heathcote's wife answering the door to the baker in the house that abutted on to the school.

She was a little woman, inclined to tubbiness, but tightly contained in her clothes. She was doing housework in a two-piece costume, protected only by a floral-patterned pinafore, which she took off at the sight of Wright as if she were ashamed of it.

She plunged into a love-hate relationship the moment that she saw him. Wright found himself the target for all worries that she had suffered through the harassment of her husband. This was the first time that she had spoken about it to anyone except Heathcote. It was the first time she had described the ashen face, coming round the wall from school day after day. She had sat, read, ironed through the oft-repeated, futile, inconclusive arguments. She had made pots of tea for them in the shivering hours of sleepless nights. She was too intelligent to think that Wright was on the side of the trouble-makers— but he was the first official to whom she had talked herself. She talked.

Wright listened to a diatribe against the world, especially the world of educational administrators, who had not the decency to accept the word of a man who was approaching an impoverished old age in their service. She inveighed against the shadow of impending retirement, with a house to buy in an inflated market. She had bit her tongue (she said) through a life of ladder-climbing that had brought her no higher than a houseful of battered furniture and a case of books, mostly about teaching children to read. Pretty soon, Wright hoped, this could all be deflected into a diatribe against Cynthia Merridew. He waited for the storm to spend itself.

"I'm sorry, Mr. Wright. I see nothing but blood-suckers."

At last, she began to cry.

"I'm sorry, Mr. Wright."

"Don't be sorry. It strikes me your husband's been holding the dirty end of the stick too long."

"Of all the sticks, Mr. Wright. It all keeps coming back to the same man."

"And now this Cynthia Merridew business."

"My husband had nothing to do with that, Mr. Wright."

"We do know that, Mrs. Heathcote."

"By the state in which he came home after you'd been talking to him yesterday, I was beginning to wonder."

"I don't remember that we pressed him unduly. Certainly we wouldn't have wanted to give that impression. Did you know Miss Merridew, Mrs. Heathcote?"

"My husband once brought her in to tea after school."

The memory did not seem to bring her any pleasure.

"What did you think of her?" Wright asked bluntly.

"What did I think of her? Mr. Wright, she's dead—cruelly and unnecessarily. What's the point of dragging things up about her?"

"It's our job to find out all we can."

"It won't help," she said, quiet and emphatic.

"Why not?"

"Only a madman would do a thing like that."

"A madman who knew a good deal about her. Somebody who had read at least one of her books."

"That was all a lot of rubbish, Mr. Wright. She would get hold of any silly yarn from any yokel in a hedge-bottom, and blow it up until it was a legend. They weren't Norfolk legends, half of them—they were Merridew inventions."

"The Dutchman's hanging wasn't."

"And wouldn't it have been better for everybody, Miss Merridew above all, if that had been forgotten?"

Wright tried a fresh approach.

"Are you a Norfolk woman, Mrs. Heathcote?"

"Born and bred in this village. And that's another thing: Walter never complains. But sometimes he just sits and looks at me, and I know what he's thinking. If I hadn't wanted to come back here—''

"So you must have known the Margerums when they were children?"

"Maurice and I were in the same class—in this building."

"Do you have much to do with them, Mrs. Heathcote?"

"Peasants, Mr. Wright."

"You're talking about Maurice, his father, Tom—and Kate? And Charlie?"

"Charlie doesn't belong to this village. The way he keeps that place—the way he keeps himself—it's a disgrace. But what can you expect? Blood will out. They should never have kept him. A lot of people will tell you that."

Wright did some rapid mental arithmetic.

"You must have known Charlie Margerum when you were a child."

"He's older than I am. He had left school before I started. That's something to be thankful for."

"Would it be true to say that Cynthia Merridew and Charlie Margerum were friends?"

"You should ask my husband that."

"Oh? Why?"

She was one of those women who took no thought for the consequences of her tongue.

"Fancy being jealous of a man like that!"

"Who is? Your husband of Charlie Margerum?"

"I've always known it. I could tell it from the look on his face. She could never get away from this school fast enough, to get herself over to Marsh Hall—''

"And that upset your husband?"

"Not that he ever said a word, you understand. But I can read him like a book. 'Good riddance,' I used to say. 'It's a blessing that there is somebody to take her off your back.' ''

"Charlie and Miss Merridew seem such an unexpected partnership," Wright said hopefully.

"Nothing was unexpected where Cynthia Merridew and a pair of trousers were concerned."

"Indeed?"

"The trouble with my husband is that he never does see things as they are. He only sees things as he thinks they ought to be. He's too good a man. He doesn't expect others to be different from himself.''

"So he was mistaken about Cynthia Merridew?''

"If you must know, Mr. Wright—she was making a set at him.''

"You're sure of that?''

"It was all over the village, Mr. Wright. Everybody knew except Walter. Even the children—ten-year-olds—were talking about the way they sat with their heads together at his desk, poring over some old map or other.''

"He didn't know about this? And yet you say he was jealous of Charlie Margerum?''

Mrs. Heathcote was taken aback, as if she were startled that her words had been taken seriously.

"There was never anything between them, Mr. Wright. I don't want you to go away from here with that impression. If I thought that, I wouldn't still be here, I do assure you.''

Wright ventured a meek reminder.

"Mrs. Heathcote—she only came here once a year.''

"I don't take a day off a year, Mr. Wright—a day's leave of my self-respect and my senses.''

And then she pleaded with him not to let her husband know of the content of their conversation.

"I don't want him to be worried by anything else, Mr. Wright.''

Wright closed his notebook and put it away. As he went through the gate from the private house into the playground, he was unable to resist the temptation to open the school door and peep into the class-room.

He did not approach Walter Heathcote—merely waved cheerily, as if greeting an old friend, then let himself out again. The headmaster smiled sadly. He was helping Pamela Tennant to make up the day's weather-chart.

·9·

So I took the spade in my own hands and showed him how to turn a spit of soil. Then, later in the afternoon, Ray Denny went away muttering to himself when I had to rebuke him for planting a row of cabbage plants so loosely that I could tweak them out with thumb and forefinger.

He is brooding and miserable. Everyone about the farm these days seems brooding and miserable. So I called him back and absolutely insisted that he tell me what was on his mind. And he tried to blame everything on to Will. "Miss, we shall have to know where we stand with him," he said. "Apples, Miss—that's all he knows anything about. And if you ask me, there's orchards in Worcestershire that aren't all they're cracked up to be."

I don't know why they hate him so. Perhaps it is because he so obviously knows more about everything than they do.

This farm used to be such a haven of happiness and prosperity. Who was that man who wrote about all the atoms spinning gaily in a well regulated universe? That's what it was always like here. Even in the years after my mother died, and my father was so sad, he wasn't really giving his mind to things the way he used to do, everything still went on steadily, quietly, predictably. And everyone respected everybody else.

Now everyone was changing in the same way. Everyone suddenly had problems of their own—and a few years ago no one had ever seemed to have a problem. Old Harriet Wells, who for years had ruled the bed-linen, the lamp oil and the servants' kitchen, who had served the Franklins as nurse-maid, governess and cook, was now complaining of arthritis in her hands, and no longer cleaned the silver. The girl who came for two hours every morning to black-lead grates and chop vegetables incredibly announced that she had taken a job at the new vegetable canning factory on the Lynn Road.

Maud shrewdly remarked that while her father was alive, everybody had seemed to love her. Now there did not even seem to be the opportunity to prove whether she was lovable or not. She struggled with possible solutions.

> *Have decided to bring back the good old custom of our Harvest Home. I probably can't bring the old days back, but at least it won't be for want of trying. How I remember those great feasts before the War—the great barn swept and clean, seats at the massive trestle-tables made from every box and packing-case that would take a covering of canvas or sacking—a scene reminiscent of Brueghel, with barrels of ale for every man to tap, and smoke-black hams, great side of beef—and huge fruit pies. And every man, woman and child who had lent the least of a hand in the fields was there—no questions asked about anyone else from the village who felt that he had a right to his knees under our board.*

Harriet Wells demurred at the cost; Maud over-ruled her. And wouldn't the men get drunk, and start fighting? There had never been a drunken fight in her father's day. But it seemed that men did not even get drunk in the same way that they used to.

Wright, reading the diary at last at a fold-down table in a corner of the wireless trailer, wondered how much liquor some of the men had put away before the festivities even started.

The first sign that things were going to excess was when Ray half stood at his place at the table and shouted something to Edward, who was over on the far side of the room. Maud did not hear the words, but there was particularly raucous laughter at several points around about. Edward answered something—again she could not make out what—and two or three men's heads, including one or two habitual trouble-makers, were turned over their owner's shoulders to try to see her reaction.

At that, Will got up from his chair—they were wedged shoulder to shoulder along where he was sitting—and he could not move without creating a minor disturbance. He made his way along the walls to where Edward was, and men, suddenly silent now, crouched down in their places to let him pass. Edward turned his head to smile at Will— insolent and challenging—whereupon Will brought down the back of his hand across Edward's mouth. He drew blood, and all the plates and cutlery danced about the table.

And Will walked out into the night. Subdued conversation began again after he had passed out through the wide double doors. The vicar rose, to begin an unnecessarily long speech of thanks to their hostess.

I was so thankful when I could decently escape, into air cool and clean, free from the dry smell of chaff, meal and old leather—and the rancid odors of all the perspiring bodies. I looked in to see how things were faring in the stable, which had been rigged out with hurricane lamps and huge tubs for the washing up.

There was no sign of Will about the outbuildings or the brick-yard. Everywhere people were coming and going, and I could see that there was no light showing through the uncurtained windows of his bunk-house. Perhaps, I thought, he has gone down to the Red Lion *in fury, or out on to the marsh in deep dudgeon. But the picture that stuck in my mind was of him, with his kit-bag on his shoulder, marching out of Mawson's Drove as solitary as he wandered in.*

But with to many people milling about, and wanting to hold me in conversation, I dared not look for him, or appear to be looking.

But I know Will Stratton too well. He is so headstrong— and yet so shy. I know he will go away, because he cannot stay and face the thought of what he has done tonight.

The Chief Inspector looked in on Wright and nodded affably enough.

"Good stuff you've got there, Sergeant?"

"Better than you'll find in most paperbacks. Especially one particular chap's."

"Kenworthy told me he'd read himself awake last night."

Looked out this morning—and Will was about his jobs in the yard as usual. But every time I tried to make an opportunity to talk to him something happened to hinder me: Ray suddenly coming up, wheeling an empty barrow; or Ray's head and shoulders popping up over a hedge, where I had not known he was.

And I so wanted to talk to Will, and put him at his ease, and let him know that I did not care two hoots what happened last night.

At the end of the day—an October day, with sparrows bathing themselves in the gray dust of the yard—her eye was on its mettle for detail—she saw him letting himself out of the barred main gate. She called him to the back door and he took off his cap and came up awkwardly.

"Will—I wanted a word with you."

Harriet Wells was fiddling with a tatting cushion at the dining-room table. She thought the exercise was good for her fingers.

"I'm not stopping you from going somewhere, Will?"

"Just down into the village, Miss. Just for a turn in the fresh air."

He was not wearing his best suit, but he had spruced himself up a little. At least, he was not carrying his bag.

"I'll come with you, if I may. Just give me a minute to get a woolly."

So they walked down the road they had first come up together from the village.

"What was all that about last night, Will?"

"Miss—I've been meaning to come up all day and apologize."

"I'm sure there's no need at all for that. I could see that you were provoked. But I want to know—what was it all about?"

"I wasn't going to tell you, Miss—but now I think I will—saving your feeling."

"I wish you would, Will."

He was ill at ease, swallowed, looked away, did not want to frame his opening sentence. Then he brought it out, fast, and in a monotone.

"These men—they're always saying—they reckon that I killed your father."

There had been no other mention in the diary of Captain Franklin's death. The vital pages had been removed—but, in any case, Wright did not think that they were given over to speculative details. The only statement they had had was from Major Tennant. He had said that Franklin had fallen on his gun—and that it seemed an unlikely thing to have happened.

"But Will, that is nonsensical. You and my father—"

"I would have followed him anywhere, Miss Maud. The good Lord above knows where I did follow him."

"I know, Will."

"And it's a well-known fact that I was nowhere near Hickling's when it happened. The Captain had sent me back up the farm for the Winchester, because the hammerless was jamming. I spoke to Barnett at the gun-store door."

"I shall speak to the men."

"It won't do any good, Miss. I'd far rather you didn't. There's no reason in them. I sometimes think—"

"Go on, Will—what do you think?"

"No, Miss—I said I would save your feelings."

"There are things that need to be said, Will."

"Then I'll say it, Miss Maud, once and for all, then neither of us need ever say it again—I sometimes think the Captain knew what he was doing, when he sent me back for another gun he didn't need. They didn't find anything wrong with the breech of the hammerless when they examined it. That was the thing I thought was going to run against me."

Kenworthy later established that a discreet coroner, often a guest at the Franklins' table, had lost no time in bringing in a verdict of accidental death.

"You mean, my father took good care to send you somewhere where you'd be seen—"

"I find that hard to escape, Miss Maud—saving your feelings."

They stopped talking, and Maud looked out to an eastern horizon where a dark gray sky was merging with the waterline.

"When people take their own lives, Will," she said at last, "the saddest thing is that everyone who knew them must ask themselves, wasn't there anything that *I* could do to make them want to stay?"

The words came to me on the spur of the moment, and they brought tears to my eyes. I turned away from Will and sobbed as I had not sobbed after either of the funerals.
Will put his arm about my shoulder.

"That's what they mean when they say a couple need each other."

"I beg your pardon?"

Wright remembered with a start that he was not alone in the office. A constable from the County H.Q. was manning a wireless console. Nothing had come in in the last hour.

"Sorry, mate," Wright said. "Talking to myself."

"Bad sign, Sarge. Like the C.I. says—good read you've got there."

"What they call a human story."

"How much longer before you go and get him?"

"Get him?"

"Charlie."

"When Kenworthy tells me to."

"They're getting up a petition in the village—asking for protection if he isn't pulled in."

"You like to go and fetch him, cock?"

"Me, Sarge?"

"Arrest him on sus, your own initiative. Hold him here till Kenworthy gets back. Make a name for yourself."

"I'd rather just sit and listen to this static."

It was too easy—perhaps a dangerous deception—to identify Will Stratton with Charlie Margerum: the physique, the careful speech, the delicate and often wounded sensibility.

Maud did not record that Will Stratton showed any natural diffidence, once his fingers had closed about her arm; nor had she thought it worth while making any notes about what steps she herself took to help him overcome his inhibitions.

The next day, she made no bones about her appearance in the yard. In full and uncurtained view of Edward and Ray, of Harriet Wells, and any other servant or neighbor who chanced to be in the offing, she interrupted Will in his work—and for a long time they leaned together over a gate and talked about the running of the farm, and what was going wrong with it.

That evening, she went to him in his bunk-house, ostensibly to take him a catalogue of equipment that they had said they would look over together. Edward and Ray had gone home. Harriet had shut herself in her room to write letters. And Will had made curtains for his window. It was the first thing she noticed when she went in; and it was the first time since he had come to Mawson's Drove that he had considered it desirable to hide from the view of anyone who might care to look in. They were nothing more than old meal-sacks, torn open and hemmed with cobbler's twine; as curtains, they were laughable—and they both laughed.

The room was clean—he scrubbed the floor every Saturday afternoon—and there was furniture of a sort—a bedside table, a stool and a shelf for soap and razor, all nailed together from old soap-boxes. The effect of the ensemble was—*the rough male kiss of blankets*; Maud was unable to resist the quotation. She did not rhapsodize about any other aspect of unbridled masculinity; but she stayed late, and there was a symbol in the margin, a capital W in a circle, that was repeated prolifically during the next few weeks.

> *Made a pair of decent curtains for the bunk-house, and hung them myself, while Will was in the fields. Told the others that henceforward they are to regard him as their foreman—news which they received in uncommenting silence.*

From foreman to baliff was a transition that had no marked delineation; but there was a marked change in the rhythm of management of the farm. A lot of rubbish went to the autumn bonfires.

> *Will is not at ease anywhere in the house beyond the kitchen. He looks at my dressing-table as if he were afraid of my bowls and brushes. He treads—or, rather, tries not to tread—on the sheep-skin rug as if he were afraid of his own feet.*

''Randy stuff you got there, Sarge?''

''Real McCoy, boy.''

''Let's have a *shufti*, when you've finished.''

''Not that sort of book, boy—privileged borrowers only.''

''Mean bastard.''

Wright dropped his eyes again to the page.

Maud put her hand on Will's shoulders.

''Will—I know you're never yourself, when you come up here. It's out of a sort of honor for my father, isn't it?''

''I can't seem to get used to things—Maud.''

''You don't even like calling me by my name, do you? Will, you've got to understand; the past has no hold on either of us any more. There's only us and the future now.''

Will wanted to believe it, but she knew he didn't.

''If you want to, Will, we'll go across the yard. Anything to make you happy and natural, Will.''

She reached for her dressing gown.

''But isn't it better in a proper bed?''

He grasped the sleeve of her night-dress.

''It's better in a bed.''

There's only us and the future now.

After the first fever, Maud's uncertainty began to show between the lines. What future could there be? Will had told her, that first evening after the Harvest Home, that he was already married; to a girl he had met on a drunken night in a pub in Malvern Wells, on leave after First Somme. She had only wanted passion, and he was in prime condition—he used the phrase himself—to lust after her. After the war, she had turned out to be a shrew, a slut, a wastrel. She laughed contemptuously at the poetry in him; he cringed in the slum to which she anchored him. He determined that she should drive him neither to drink nor self-destruction. When he reached the stage of knowing that he must murder her if he stayed, he remembered the code of Captain Franklin, packed his bag, and walked across the Shires to the Marshes.

''She'll divorce you. I don't mind the publicity. I'll be glad—''

''She'll never divorce me.''

''Is she a Catholic?''

"Out of spite she'll not divorce me."

"She might want to marry again herself."

"I wouldn't bet on that."

"We can make it worth her while. I'll go and see her."

"No, Maud, no. No, no, no, no, no."

"Well—what does it matter? The farm's mine. I can live here in any style or fashion that I choose. Surely you're not still brooding on what my father would have thought? I tell you, my father would have been *glad*—he *knew* you—"

"We've still got to live, Maud. We've got to be sensible."

"Come to bed, darling."

Capital W in a circle. For all their urgency, there were complexities of discretion in the early days. But they might as well have lived and loved without pretence. With complacent looks on their faces, with a silence about their thoughts that was more insolent than speech, Ray and Edward announced that they had found other jobs. The same day, Harriet Wells, prim, her chin quivering, said there were things which it was not for her to say. Maud headed her off from saying them, and told her that there was no need for her to stay to work out her notice. Even the latest girl who was peeling potatoes and sifting ash said that she was leaving. At least, she did not warrant a gratuity. Maud was very generous in her treatment of Harriet Wells, and Harriet thanked her, sincerely and surprised, but without any relaxation of her accusing features.

So now there were people at large and discharged from responsibility who could confirm and embroider what the village had already surmised. Hadn't Kenworthy spotted the probability—at least as probable as any chance of finding Will Stratton—that Ray and Edward still took their nightly pints in the *Red Lion*? Even the girl from the kitchen sink might still be in Mawson's Drove. Or was that what the Old Man had meant when he had said that the answer was in the book?

"Come to a boring bit, Sarge?"

"There are no boring bits in this book, China."

"That Major chap's here."

"Tennant? Where?"

"Just been shown into the C.I.'s office."

Wright closed his book and stretched out his arm for his raincoat.

But already the C.I. was looking around the door.

"Going somewhere, Sergeant?"

"There are some ploys that the Superintendent left me to do."

"I know all about that—"

His tone was accommodating, but had the beginning of testiness. Perhaps Wright had been a little hasty in his judgment of this cove. He'd played the game up to now.

"That bloody soldier's here again. Wants to hand over a petition demanding the arrest of his brother-in-law—and says he has additional evidence. You know these personalities better than I do. You've seen *all* the evidence, being a full-fledged sergeant. I'd like you to sit in with me and act as long-stop—forward short leg, if you like."

This was more than reasonable—but the other opportunity was heaven-sent.

"Sir—this is just—"

"I'm quite sure that Kenworthy—"

"It isn't that, sir. My instructions are to talk to Mrs. Tennant as soon as I can isolate her from her husband. I've been wondering all morning how I could pull that off."

"If you must, you must, I suppose."

"Sir—"

"Something else, Sergeant?"

"Sir—the longer you can hang on to him, the better for me."

"Oh? She's as nice as that, is she? Come and see me when we're both through, will you? It can take me a long time to take a man's statement when I feel like it."

·10·

"I'M SORRY, MR. Wright, you've just missed my husband. He's gone over to your H.Q. with some new evidence."

So Wright did not even have to tell her that it was not her husband he had come to see. She offered him coffee, and seemed not entirely averse to his company.

"What new evidence is this, then, Mrs. Tennant?"

She was still inclined to be nervous, her eyes restless, weighing her words as if afraid of every intonation.

"I'm sure if you cared to wait half an hour, my husband would much rather tell you with his own lips."

"Has he been carrying out an investigation of his own, then?"

"I'd rather you waited, Mr. Wright."

Wright let his eyes wander round the room: the typewriter, still in mid-action, a fresh sheet on the roller, barely started. He looked again at the photograph of the Margerums, and the portrait of Kate's mother. Kate Tennant noticed the direction of his glance and the intensity of his study.

"You did not know her, Mr. Wright. How much can a photograph tell you?"

Wright wondered: the stylized pose, the skin that did not need cosmetics, the intelligent brow, the melancholy eyes. How much of the revelation of the diary would he have forecast from that profile?

"I'd be interested—"

Kate Tennant did her best to smile. Side-tracked from what she took to be the main issue, she was more relaxed.

"Give me a character-study of her, Mr. Wright—all that you see there."

"I'd say that she was basically a romantic. That she took

even slight shades of meaning deeply to heart. That she was passionate of nature. Loyal to her feelings—capable of throwing all other considerations to the winds for the sake of what she knew to be right. Consequently there'd be period of high elation—to compensate for moods of deep depression. I think she was obstinate to the point of bed-rock firmness on issues that didn't seem to mean a thing to those about her.''

And now Kate Tennant actually laughed.

"Which only goes to show how wrong even a policeman can be."

"You think so?"

"Mr. Wright, you could not be further from the mark. A romantic? Well, perhaps in the odd restful moment. She liked romantic reading—when family and farm gave her any time for books. But all those other things you said. Passionate? She was a disciplined woman. Every moment of her training had been just that. She was a well-to-do farmer's daughter, Mr. Wright—''

Like the Colonel's lady? But Mrs. Tennant had only been a Major's lady.

"Oh—I know she had been misled in her youth—''

"I am not judging her by that."

"In her father's homestead, she preserved the graces. She did the same for my father and for us—only it was a different time, a different world. Whatever her feelings were, she had been taught from childhood that they did not matter. And as for obstinacy on points of principle—I can't imagine what sort of life you think my parents led! My father attended to all matters of business. She would not have dreamed of trying to interfere.''

"Wouldn't you have thought that there would be—well—misplaced guilt-complexes?''

"Guilt complexes, Mr. Wright? You make her sound like a psychopath. What had she to feel guilty about? Because she had been imposed upon?''

"Some people are not always reasonable in all matters.''

"My mother was reasonable at all times, Mr. Wright. To hear you talk, you'd think we all qualified for the madhouse. I suppose it comes from having to spend so much of your time with aberrations and abnormalities. We are all normal people, Mr. Wright.''

"Including Charlie?"

"I've nothing against Charlie. I find a good deal in him to admire. You must expect our relationship with him to have been a little different."

"In what way was it different, Mrs. Tennant?"

"I don't know why you're asking me all this. I'm not sure that you have the right to. If you will wait until the Major comes home—"

"The Major. No; perhaps I have no right. But I do happen to think it's relevant. And I do happen to be personally interested."

"Our relationship was different, because Charlie was different. You can't deny that, from the evidence of your own eyes."

"All the same, I'd be interested in your analysis of the difference."

"All right, then, you shall have it: Charlie is deceitful, eccentric, cruel—including animals and birds—dishonest, immoral, lazy, feckless and dirty."

"But you will find something in him to admire?"

To this she did not reply.

"The fact is, isn't it, Mrs. Tennant, that you and your brothers—and perhaps your father more than most—have always regarded Charlie's very existence as having defiled your mother?"

He half expected her to say, "Well, hasn't it?" but for the moment she was too angry. Then her own training asserted itself.

"Mr. Wright—I can understand your having been impressed in a certain way by my half-brother. He is—can be—plausible. But you have no idea what has been lavished on him: the settlement of that very big farm, that he's allowed to run derelict; interest-free loans from my father, of which he's never repaid a penny; the hours my brother Tom has spent with him over his accounts—if you can call them accounts."

"They also let him go to prison."

"He had only himself to blame for that. Why are you so interested in something that is over and paid for?"

"It is the kind of thing that is more easily forgotten by those who stand right outside it."

"Precisely what do you mean by that?"

"I mean that if my name were Charlie Margerum, I perhaps wouldn't forget quite as easily as some people would like me to."

"Charlie has had his last drop of blood from that pound of flesh, I do assure you."

Wright knew that he was winning. He provoked her further.

"One minute you say you admire him—to show me that you have no ill feelings. Now you're leaning over backwards to show me what a bad lot your brother is.

"Half-brother."

"Even in that insistence, you betray your state of mind."

"Mr. Wright, who else in this village could have done such a thing as has been done? Who else was as thick with Cynthia Merridew as he was? What sort of filth was it they were getting up to together? Who made the scaffold? Who took those sadistic cine pictures of her, pretending to be hanged? Did you ever hear of such insanity? With whom did she spend four hours on Monday afternoon? And what are you doing about it? You are foisting yourself on decent people, asking insolent and irrelevant and intensely personal questions about the past—while he has just gone out fishing. Why he isn't under lock and key, none of us can understand."

"Because wrongful arrest does not go down well with those we have to answer to."

"If you're so frightened of putting a foot forward, it's a wonder that you ever dare to move your feet at all."

"And can you give me a single working paragraph of proof?"

"Who else could have done it?"

And Wright thought rapidly. Should he plunge? Should he risk telling her too much? Should he risk putting something in her mind that might jeopardize a trap that Kenworthy might soon want to set?

He felt sure that Kenworthy, given the opening, would have taken the chance.

"Who else could have done it, Mrs. Tennant? Hundreds of people. But we are beginning to narrow it down. We think it must be someone who knows enough about the past to swing it, oh so naturally, on to Charlie."

"If you think that, then you must be living in some land beyond the skies."

"I wouldn't let it worry you," Wright said, in mock comfort. "There are other people in the village to whom it might apply, besides the Margerums."

"I don't know how you dare—!"

Wright smiled, in very effective imitation of his master.

"Mr. Wright—I shall have to ask you—"

"Think about it, Mrs. Tennant. Try to see this village as an outsider might."

"You are trying to be too clever. Mr. Wright—you are trying to see too much. You say you want evidence. Well, I'll tell you: that's just what my husband is doing now, over at your headquarters. He is giving Mr. Kenworthy all the evidence you could possibly need. Evidence of two men who saw my half-brother in the small hours of Tuesday night, driving his van and trailer, with a bundle and the scaffold, down to the spot on the Leam where he moors his dinghy. And from there he rowed up to the culvert in the seawall, helped by the rising tide—and towing the scaffold behind him."

Wright tried—he thought successfully—not to look abashed.

"You could have told me this half an hour ago."

"My husband preferred to take it to the man in charge."

"Two men? Two local men? Out and about in the mist in the small hours of Tuesday night?"

"The Major has the details. So has Mr. Kenworthy, by now. I am saying no more."

Wright did not bother to tell her that Kenworthy was not here. He knew it would not be many minutes now before the Major was back, and he had no great desire for the untidiness of a confrontation that he could avoid.

But he had a ludicrous desire to go over and see what was on the typewriter this morning. He wondered what kind of diffuse lighting was falling on the soft down of whose cheek now.

·11·

"THAT SEEMS TO be that," the Chief Inspector said. "I only hope Kenworthy's not going to be away too long. I don't see what power on earth can stop him from pulling in Charlie now."

"Kenworthy is usually the only power on Kenworthy's earth."

"It's up to him, then. He said this was going to happen. 'Sometime, during the course of the day,' he said, 'somebody's going to come in with irrefutable evidence that can't leave us any alternative to clapping a hand on Charlie's shoulder. You're to leave him alone. Under no circumstances and on no pretext whatsoever are you to interfere with him till I get back.' And, thank God, he put that in writing in the log."

"These two witnesses—"

"Poachers."

"At this time of year, and on that kind of night? There's nothing on the marsh but ducks and geese."

"Poaching is a highly commercialized affair these days. Bulk loads to London markets. Scientific, too. Doped bait, to make the birds easy to pick up at night. Nothing new in it really, Sergeant. In the old days, the local yobbos used to use raisins soaked in whiskey. They stuck in the birds' throats. Modern methods are more reliable—and less wasteful."

"But most of the stuff's out of season."

"Not if it's sold out of deep freeze. And they don't ask questions in some sections of the hotel trade."

"These were local men?"

"No."

"So how has Tennant got on to them?"

"He fancies himself as a sporting type. He's often on the

marshes in the winter dawn. On the edge of town, anyway. He says he overheard a conversation between these two—and made them come forward.''

"It seems to me, sir, that this corner of the country was unusually thickly populated on Tuesday night."

"Five people in twenty square miles, to my reckoning. One of them now dead. It's feasible, Sergeant."

"It's feasible, sir. It's feasible that every able-bodied man in the village was up all night in the swamp."

"Don't pitch the probability too low, Sergeant. There *are* poachers operating this stretch of country. I've had a case in mid-stream for months that I ought to be working on this very minute. And if anybody is thinking of monkey business in the reeds, then that Mawson's Leam culvert is the obvious approach. And it does happen to give you an uninterrupted view of the flank of Charlie's territory."

"There's something about this that I don't like."

"Nor I. If it weren't for what Kenworthy said, I'd find it all too easy."

"If Kenworthy's right, this new testimony must be false. And if Tennant thought the testimony was false, would he have forced it forward like this?"

"What are you arguing, Sergeant?"

"That if the testimony's false, Tennant brought it to us in good faith."

"Or is that just what he wants us to think? I see that you prefer to look on Tennant as a villain. I agree with you. He's what we used, in my vulgar youth, to call a shit. But that might not be relevant."

"We just sit tight, then."

"That's it, Sergeant. And let's thank God we can. And Sergeant—if you do pick up anything new in the course of the day, keep me posted. I'll do the same for you."

"Fair do's, sir."

A ploughman's lunch in the *Red Lion* was both appropriate and appetizing, though it was doubtful how long the supply of French bread and continental Cheddar was likely to hold out. There were a few locals among the press of policemen, police auxiliaries, journalists and week-day sightseers. And because of this, the locals, despite their reputation for suspicion, taciturnity and introversion, were talking loudly.

"Like father like son."

"Do you remember the time he started a fight at the Harvest Home?"

"There used to be a lot of money changed hands on Saturday nights at Charlie's place."

"That there did. They were coming from Norwich, Swaffham, Ipswich."

"London," one of them said. "There were plenty of them came from London."

A glass was emptied with theatrical finality and a reporter signed to the landlord that he was buying the next round. A lot was going into brains and notebooks for which the press could find no immediate use. But when the season for checkbook headlines was declared open by an arrest, there was going to be a run on the past.

"Do you know she once had the nerve to take him to church with her?"

"My mother was there that night. She said the congregation didn't know where to look. Stunned they were—stunned."

"Then he walked out on her."

"Soon as he'd had what he wanted."

"Used to quarrel up there, night-times. You could hear it down the road."

"Pots and pans flying about."

The landlord phoned the Cash-and-Carry to book fresh supplies. The landlady put on her coat to drive and fetch them.

Wright picked up the diary and went back to the compound.

·12·

CAPITAL W IN a circle. Throughout the late autumn they had the house and land to themselves. Maud made one or two attempts to set on fresh labor—but the village was massed against her. One woman did agree to come up two mornings a week to help with the cleaning—but she was such a sloven, and made such long ears for any remark to carry back to the gossips—even asking pointed and provocative questions—that Maud sacked her on her first pay-day.

After that, they said they would manage. And the season was kind to them. The first light ground-frost did not make itself felt until late in November; but even then the sun, weak but effective, was shining by mid-morning. The kitchen-door stood always open.

And Will seemed to have lost—at no discernible point in time—his inhibitions about coming into the house. Both worked hard at the things that needed to be done—Maud in the house, throwing out the accumulation from her parents' lives that she could now face up to without sentimental obstacles. There was an old painted copper tea-urn, with a tap at the bottom and a tessellated lid, that she had always hated. It held two gallons, stood on the dining-room sideboard, and was the ugliest object in creation.

She threw it out one morning, right across the yard, in a great triumphant arc, from the kitchen door to a heap of debris that was piling up in a corner. Will, painting a barn door a yard or two from where it landed, looked back over his shoulder and grinned. The man who sold paraffin and clothes-pegs and baking tins and tea-cloths from a shop-windowed van drove up at that moment, and was able to report violence.

There was no strict demarcation into spheres of activity. In an old skirt, a pullover and a shirt of her father's, open at the neck, she helped to renew a long stretch of chicken-wire. Together they dug, milked cows—and found the time to walk the fields to set traps for vermin. And love was where the moment took them. They were in bed by eight many an evening. Capital W in a circle. But of all the places where they made love, Maud herself began to prefer the curtained shed. They went back there even when a chill was on the evening, and Will broke sticks and lit a fire in the iron stove.

One week-end the relatives from Ely came—Uncle Robert (Gordon) and the aunt who preferred her sandwiches with crusts.

Without discussing the matter, Will made himself scarce about duties on the perimeter of the farm. He did not come in to lunch—and when she came to look for him during the Sunday afternoon—because her uncle had expressed the desire to meet her bailiff—he was nowhere to be found. He had taken himself for a long walk along the tide-line.

She chided him for it afterwards—but she had done nothing more herself than keep up a pretence. She asked herself whether she would have shown an honest face to her relatives if Will had been with her to help to brazen it out. Her uncle was one of those worrying men, tied to the patterns that had always been, who desperately wanted to look at her account books, but had not quite the nerve to ask outright. And her aunt asked questions about Harriet Wells, the neighbors and the people in the village, to which she gave answers that were transparently evasive. They pressed her to spend Christmas at Ely.

But this she resisted with every rationalization to which she could lay her mind. Christmas loomed large among the promises that she and Will held out for themselves.

But Will was not happy over her determination to take her with him to the midnight service in the parish church. It was not that he had any objection to the church as such—he reckoned that he was as good a Christian as any that sat in a pew.

"But it wouldn't be right."

"And why wouldn't it be right?"

"It can do nothing but add to your difficulties."

"*Our* difficulties, Will. When we face the world, we face it together."

"Unfortunately, we aren't in much of a state to face it together, Maud."

"What rot and rubbish! Haven't we come together in the purest, the most consuming, the most *honest* way that a man and woman can? If we run away from the world, then the world has every right to chase us from the pack. If we *face* up to them, they will accept us in due time—and it won't be long, you'll see, before that will be. In any case, the village isn't the world."

I managed to persuade him. Again he put on that dark suit, that looks as if it belongs to a different century, and we walked together up the crunching drive between the moonlit headstones. When we first took our seats in the Franklin pew, there was a hassock lying between us. We sat like this, silent for some minutes. Then I picked it up and put it on the floor. The foot-rail rattled. The organist was playing the Pastoral Symphony from Bach's Christmas Oratorio. Then I moved up, so that my shoulder was up against his arm. You could feel the utter absence of whispering, anywhere in the church.

The vicar, raising well-manicured fingers to intone the Bidding Prayer, seemed to wait, uncertain whether to begin, looking down at her: round, tortoiseshell spectacles and a conventional, cruel mouth.

Going out through the Norman porch, she tightly clasped Will's arm. They passed a knot of people who seemed to be ignoring them—and then there was an unexpected voice, she did not know whose it was.

"Good night, Miss Maud."

She returned the greeting.

"A merry Christmas. Compliments of the season to you."

Pin-points of frost sparkled up from the flag-stones. The air was sharp in their lungs. They crossed fields rutted with black shadows. The house was suddenly warm, the sprigs of holly behind the pictures were theirs, not part of someone else's festivity. They did not go out to the bunkhouse that night. There was not time.

On Christmas morning, they breakfasted late and hugely—thick gammon rashers, eggs and mountains of potato. Maud gave Will a Roll's Razor, self-stropping in a shining metal case. He gave her a penny for it, so that it should not cut their friendship. And he gave her a wooden courting spoon, elaborately carved, after the fashion of his part of the country, with their initials woven in an intricate monogram.

Sad to say we were quarrelling angrily by the middle of the morning. Will is finding it increasingly difficult not to be always looking on the black side. He was sitting in the kitchen, watching me put the final touches to our Christmas dinner. He has killed us a gosling—a turkey would be too big for us—and I was just putting the finishing touches to the trussing, threading the string through the drum-sticks.

"After the roast," he said, "the devilled bones. And after the devilled bones—whatever's left."

"Oh, Will—what a time to be talking like that."

"I have to think. One of us has to think."

"Meaning that I never do, I suppose."

"I aren't saying that. I know when it comes to thinking— real thinking—you could lose me ten times over. But it keeps rolling round my head, what's going to happen."

"And what *is* going to happen, Will? I hope we're going to continue to make each other very, very happy."

She turned the bird over, and began to brush lard over the breast.

"Supposing—just suppose—that I was to get you with child."

She laughed, with aggressive immodesty.

"I can't imagine that either of us could be trying much harder on that score."

"It's all right laughing—"

"You nearly said *Miss Maud*, didn't you? You can give me a hand with the potatoes, Will."

He sprang readily for the peeling-knife.

"You're too pessimistic, Will."

"There are things that aren't right."

"Do you want us to stop, then?"

For a second they could hear the ticking of the clock, the

simmering of the steamer, in which the pudding-basin was done up in a cloth.

"No, Maud—I don't want us stop. If we stopped, what else would there be? But I sometimes think that we shall have to."

"Nonsense!"

"It isn't nonsense."

"If the worst comes to the worst, we can live as man and wife. Hundreds of couples—"

"And be the cast-outs of the village? Like last night? When people were only wishing us good-night so that they could push us further out into the cold?"

"Will—you're too sensitive to live. I can sell this place. It'll fetch a massive price. We can move somewhere else— somewhere where we aren't known. We can buy a property that's not too big for us to manage."

"No, Maud."

"No, Maud, No, Maud. Every time I suggest a rational solution, that's all you can say. No, Maud."

"This is your home. It was your father's home."

"And?"

"I haven't the right to deprive you of what's been yours from birth."

"You're not a batman now, Will."

"No—and I sometimes wish I were."

She saw the hurt in his eyes, wiped her hands on a cloth and put them on his shoulders.

"Will, I didn't mean that. Great God, I didn't mean it— Will, let's—not have any dinner. Let's go to bed."

"No, Maud."

"No, Will? No?"

She taunted him playfully.

"Am I growing old and haggish already, then?"

"That's not what I meant, Maud."

"Then why don't you say what you do mean?"

She did not seem able to stop herself from hurting him. But their strife was momentarily stilled by the sound of horses' hooves by the back door.

It was young Joe Margerum, jodhpurs and shining boots, hitching up his mare to a fencing post, carrying an ivory-handled crop in one hand, and a Christmas package for Maud in the other.

She undid the wrappings with suitable murmurs of anticipation. And it was a hand-made work box, inlaid with marquetry: the curve of the coast, with a sailing-boat on the sky-line and a gull sweeping down to a leaning groyne.

She asked Joe into the dining room for a sherry—and wanted Will to come in and join them. But this he would not do. He hung about at first in the kitchen, and then went over to his shed. It was some time after Joe had gone before he came back again.

"Well, there's no need for you to look so down in the mouth," she said. "I haven't eloped with him."

"You'd be better off with him than ever you will with me."

"Will—I don't even like the man. Can't stand him, in fact. He represents everything I want to get away from. I'd rather have your clogs on my hearth-rug than his cavalry boots, any day of the week. Do you know what his conversation consists of? Hares that he missed and hares that he didn't. What beef was fetching on the hoof last Tuesday at Lynn, and how many swedes per acre he's had from the top field since he marled it the autumn before last."

Will picked up the work-box and looked at it critically.

"The trouble is," he said. "I'd never have thought of a thing like this."

Which won him a warm kiss on his cheek. And they ate their dinner together, followed by a circled W which, Wright thought, must have been somnolent and warm. She did not say whether they got up again that day.

Then Maud went to Lynn to talk to the family solicitor about putting Candle Mere Farm up for auction. She came home disappointed. He had not been charmed with the idea of her doing anything with the land except allow some colorlessly reliable expert to manage it for her. He could not, of course, prevent her from doing anything she wanted with it. But there was the complication that probate on her father's will had not yet been granted, though this could surely only now take a matter of weeks. There was nothing, naturally, to prevent the property from being put on the market at once, if that was what she wanted, but no decision could be taken without the approval of the executors—one of whom was Uncle Robert.

So she had to wait—and she was impatient for a decision. A matter of a few weeks suddenly yawned like an eternity.

And winter set in. For three days a blizzard blew dune-edged drifts up to the ridge-bars of the hen-houses, and then for a fortnight everything froze over. There were prodigies of snow-ridding to be done, drinking water to be carted out to birds and animals, bales to be lugged out to inaccessible corners. The cold became intense. An icicle the thickness of a man's thigh hung down from the broken guttering of the bunk-house. Will moved permanently into the house—which made, by now, only a nominal difference to their way of life. But he insisted on clearing a pathway up to the bunk-house door, so that no casual caller should infer that he was not using it.

Whatever stories visitors did carry back into Mawson's Drove with them—and every pair of eyes was restless for evidence of one kind or another—it soon became known that the couple were at each other's throats for much of the time. Their voices seemed permanently raised. *If you loved me as much as you say you do* became Maud's standby call. And Will began to threaten that he would have to go.

There was one basic question on which the couple did not disagree. Ever since he had walked into the Drove on the night of the neap-tide, he had been sending thirty shillings a week home to his wife in Worcestershire, and had been putting five shillings into a savings account which he had opened for his son. He proposed to go on doing this until he had heard that the woman had taken up with some other man; and until the boy's twenty-first birthday. And Maud agreed eagerly. She thought that his settlement on Dora was unduly generous—but he insisted that that was what he would have been handing to her if he were living with her. Maud did not press the point; she was relieved to think that Will's conscience was salved on one issue at least—and for herself, too, there was the comfortable feeling that the past had been bought off. She wanted to increase Will's wages by the amount that he was sending home. She could well afford to; it would strengthen her feeling of guiltlessness in the matter of the deserted wife; and when Will demurred, she found other little ways of making extra payments to him.

But what she could not understand—and what became the frequent cause of unpleasantness between them—was Will's apparent unwillingness to make the necessary journey into Worcestershire to try to come to some arrangement with the woman.

He agreed in principle to do so—but every time a week-end departure was almost upon him, he found some plausible reason to remain in Norfolk: a heavy fodder delivery pending, or a lambing ewe.

Whenever he did decide to stay at home after all, Maud had to admit that she was relieved. She did not relish the twenty-four hours' anxiety, wondering whether he would, in fact, ever come back to her at all. She could not rid the back of her mind of that image of his first arrival, the transitory nature of his enigmatic figure, that wilfulness of his that might, but for her astringent presence, suddenly come to some staunch and immovable decision for all the wrong reasons.

Wilful: she drew ironical attention in her diary to the accidental pun.

So Saturday mornings came and went, and he was still with her in the afternoon. And it was always mid-week before she remembered to upbraid him for his indecision.

"I'll go the week-end after next. We can't manage this Saturday. If I don't get the roof on the new brooder-shed, we're going to be behind with the hatching."

"It will wait a day or two."

"The trouble *is*, I don't like leaving you," he said honestly.

"And I don't like the thought of your going. But we've got to face up to this. You've got to go, Will, and you've got to try."

"I know."

Then suddenly he broke out.

"And what a waste of time it will be. And I know I shan't be able to answer for myself, the first time I hear her open her mouth again."

"You'll take it in your stride. It's for us, Will."

"That I know full well."

"Then I utterly fail to see what an intelligent man—"

"There's no need to go calling my intelligence into question."

"I'm not saying anything of the kind."

"I know I've not been what you call educated."

"Will—will you just listen for one moment? I know you probably won't get anywhere, but at least you've got to try."

"There are times when I wish I had just gone off into the unknown."

"And never met me?"

"And there are times when I think it would be best for me to go off into the unknown even now."

"And send me thirty shillings a week and five bob for the child?"

He was slow to see the implication of her words. She had to spell it out for him. For some days now she had thought that she was pregnant; yesterday, she was sure.

It was difficult now to be absolutely sure of the sincerity of her diary. But there was no doubting what she wanted to feel.

Prelude, Fugue and now Toccata! I am pregnant! Somewhere within me there's a little creature—oh, so ironically nothing more than an embryonic little fish—and it is part of him! Somewhere within me there is a little part of Will. Perhaps this will make things easier.

Oh! Frabjous day! Calloo! Callay!

But Will did not quote from *Jabberwocky*. He was unable to say anything at first.

"Aren't you going to tell me how happy you are?"

"Of course I'm happy, Maud."

"Is that all you can say?"

"I'm happy for you, if you want it that way."

"Of course I want it this way. Haven't I said so all along? Haven't we both said so?"

"I'm just as pleased as you are."

"You sound it!"

"Just give me a chance to think things out."

"What have you been doing all these months?"

But she knew the damage she was doing.

I knew the wickedness of my words before even my tongue had shaped them. I knew that he was not the man to think as I did—to think more slowly, anyway—to come to the same conclusions in his own good time. And I knew that the things I was saying to him were recklessly cruel and untrue. And yet I went on saying them. Why? Should I be so wildly disappointed because a man does not spontaneously share a woman's innermost feelings? Why can

*I not be as sweetly reasonable with Will as I am with a
pen on a page of white, lined paper?*

"I suppose you really will be up and away now," she said.
"and find somebody else's daughter whose father you knew
in the army."

"No—I shall never leave you now, Maud."

"But if this hadn't happened, you'd almost settled on the
time of your departure?"

"I don't understand you, Maud—I honestly don't understand
you."

"Will—I don't understand myself."

Reconciliations were becoming more difficult. The farm was
so extensive that when he was wounded beyond endurance, or
when her mood was so refractory that her company was not
safe, he could betake himself to hidden corners with a canvas
bag of tools in his hand, and be lost to her for hours at a stretch.

But reconciliations still found a place in her diary. He went,
once, out into the marshes, with a gun under his arm, and a
handful of cartridges in his pocket, a figure with shoulders that
were beginning to stoop, looking right, left and ahead of himself, but never behind. She followed him, determined to submit,
to say no more that was hurtful, to become his silent, dogged,
unprotesting, common law wife and never provoke him again
for the rest of his days, if she could only recapture the spirit
in which they had dreamed their first dreams together.

If only I could learn to keep my lips sealed.

And in another place, she was more honest with herself.

*It seems to me that I had more respect for him in the
days when he was an unknown—and I was so certain that
he was all I needed. I am still certain that he is all I need.
I know that it is only the uncertainty of the immediate
future that is getting on our nerves.*

His stride was too long for her that night—and it was many
months since she had walked in rough country. She waited for
him to come back, and fell in step with him as he came along
the edge of the creek. As she came up alongside he broke open

the breech of the gun under his arm. And for a very long time neither of them spoke—or even acknowledged the other's presence. Then at last she slipped her hand into his. He squeezed has fingers, and that night he made love to her for the first time for some weeks. But, although her pregnancy was still young, he was so afraid of her body that he was able to do neither of them justice.

They quarreled again, of course—frequently and bitterly. But they could never understand how the news of their relationship traveled so regularly to the village, the nearest house of which was almost half a mile away. But signs of people's knowledge came back to Maud's ears in peculiar ways: a chance remark from some woman who came collecting for a flag-day; a joke—at least, it could be passed off as such, if the truth did not apply—by a man who came for an installment on an insurance policy. It struck Maud that Will—who was less firmly anchored to the farm than she was, and who sometimes went down to the *Red Lion* for a drink—must have a good deal of banter to put up with.

And then, one way or another, things seemed to get better between them. He learned not to be hurt by her onslaughts, and she to control them. He said one day that he really would go back to Worcestershire and get things squared up.

"One day soon. Next week. For certain."

And she knew that now he meant it. There was a certain tone of promise that he did not break.

The lawyer wrote that the Probate Division had finished its labors on her father's estate. He wanted an appointment for her to go down and sign papers. She and Will began to discuss an asking price for Candle Mere Farms. From being a rebel thought, the idea of a common law marriage became taken for granted by both of them. There seemed, after all, to be nothing so stridently shameful about it. Much though she hated the idea of leaving the Norfolk coast, she had the feeling that once they were free of this house, this yard, this village—once they were in a community that knew nothing of their antecedents—they could start living like respectable people. They looked at advertisements in the trade papers—small-holdings rather than farms—something that they could work happily and usefully between them, with comfort assured by investing what was left of her capital. There was a place in Devon that they rather fancied; another in Cheshire, alongside the Dee estuary—*Oh! Mary! Go and call the cattle home—*

There was no doubting the practical optimism behind these entries—and Wright did not doubt that it was an optimism that Will Stratton was beginning to share. The winter of their discontent was over. A few strokes of a few pens, and they could drive into a realization of their hopes in nothing more exotic than a furniture-van.

Then came the night of the neap-tide. It was another evening in May. She wanted the salt air, the cool wind on her face, the live grasses around her ankles. Will was made happy by her new vein of vigor, her eagerness again for the things that she had always loved. She said that there would be coming a time soon when she would perhaps no longer be feeling like long walks. He grinned, and said that there was no need to make excuses. If she wanted to go, he would come with her.

But he did not come. He had been to Lynn Market that morning and bought half a dozen beef cattle, and the drover, a drunken little wretch, had still not appeared with them by early evening. At half past six, he said that she had better set out without him, if she was not to miss the best of the light. He would meet her on her way home. She was to be sure to come back along the back of the Leam.

She went. But she never wrote down her impressions of that neap-tide. When she reached the Leam outfall on her homeward lap, Will was not in sight. She began to walk briskly along the edge of the channel. There was a shiver in the air—it was by no means as hospitable a night as that other she remembered. Perhaps the drover was very late; perhaps he had still not come at all. She arrived to find the house unlit and deserted. The new bullocks were in the rough pasture. There was no sign anywhere of Will.

The place was so deserted! But there were so many possible emergencies that he might have had to attend to.

Perhaps he has screwed up his courage on the spur of the moment and gone to Malvern Wells.

But surely he would have left a note—

There was much agonized writing in the pages that followed. It was days—giving him time to return from Worcestershire—

before she admitted the thought that he might have left her. But this was only implicit in what she wrote. Never did she crystallize it into words. It was a long time now since there had been any appreciable difference between them. They were so near now to all they wanted.

She went to see the Police Sergeant—who was acutely embarrassed. Will was a free man, and if he chose to go, he could go—as he had come. But the Sergeant was discreet and kindly. He put it in a roundabout way that she ought to have a good look round the house to make sure that nothing valuable was missing.

"But isn't there anything you can *do*, Sergeant?"

"I don't see that there is, Miss Franklin. This is a free country. Our friend has broken no laws, to the best of our knowledge."

"But unofficially?"

"Unofficially—well, unofficially—you wouldn't happen to have an address in Worcestershire, I suppose?"

She had. She had brought it with her—and a woman's name, on a slip of paper.

But unofficially, when she saw the Sergeant again, a week or so later, there was nothing. He gave her the names of two or three men who, he happened to know, would be only too happy to be taken on as laborers.

"Now."

In the bunk-house, there was nothing. Will's soap and towel had gone, also his Roll's Razor and his little square of mirror. So had his kit-bag. Under his straw-mattress there lay the sombre Sunday suit.

And in the margin against this entry there was a double line in pencil and a faint exclamation mark. Kenworthy.

Of course, Wright saw. If knowledge of character meant anything, if Will Stratton had not meant to come back, he would never have left that suit of clothes behind him.

Unless—

Perhaps his Edwardian black had come to symbolize something that he did not want to remember. Perhaps Maud Franklin had been deluding herself about his state of mind—

And then Wright thought of something else. He hoped that Kenworthy might have overlooked it.

He turned to the wireless operator.

''Can you get through to G.P.O. records for me? There's an account, in a boy's name, born about 1924—''

''In Malvern Wells,'' the operator said.

''Kenworthy on to it?''

''First thing this morning. The reply came through while you were at lunch.''

He fished about in a wire basket.

''William Arthur Stratton, 6, Edge Hill, Malvern Wells, Worcestershire. Registered Number, etc., Last deposit 17th May, 1926. Holder's whereabouts unknown. Credit balance confidential, but could be made available on Home Office application.''

''That clinches it,'' Wright said.

''I suppose you know what it's all about.''

Wright thought he did. That child's account was the last thing that Will Stratton would have abandoned—unless he had come to the stage of needing a clean break from everything. Or unless he was dead. And this made sense in all directions. There were a number of men who might have felt a sense of cosmic purpose in murdering Will Stratton—among them Edward Whybrow, Ray Denny and Joe Margerum. Joe Margerum.

Someone who knew enough to frame Charlie.

Joe Margerum—

And Cynthia Merridew must have arrived at last at the same conclusion.

Then Wright remembered that Kenworthy was at this moment crossing country to fetch Will Stratton—

·13·

So what was there going to be to show Kenworthy for a day's work? Wright, doing a quick summary of his notes decided that, an hour after lunch, he knew about as much as Kenworthy had known at breakfast-time—except for the confirmation of the Post Office account. And that was going to come as no surprise.

So was your detective-sergeant really necessary? Was there anything in the morning's labor or the afternoon's prospects that was going to advance the inquiry in any way?

And what next? Isolate the women, Kenworthy had said, so isolate the women it had to be. If Kenworthy arrived back unexpectedly, and one of the women had not been isolated, the repercussions were likely to be memorable. It was likely to be inflated into the one omission on which the case depended.

Find out whether Mavis Margerum was anything more than a pudding. Charming.

Sally Margerum, now—she was a different proposition. Wright took some consolation from the prospect of an hour or so with Tom's wife. A spell with the likes of her would make a break in any week.

Full stop. It was a waste of time. An hour's argy-bargy: pleasant back-chat, parry and thrust around the crucial points, the whole underlain by a certain sexy consciousness that neither of them would admit. Wright suddenly lost his taste for that, too. Perhaps he was growing old. Perhaps, after the Franklin diaries, the lives of prosperous young couples with their feet firmly rooted in the present decade seemed a trifle unreal.

He would rather have been looking about the village for Edward and Ray, disentangling other miscellaneous gossipers from the hands of the press—perhaps even having a go at the

two poachers who claimed to have seen Charlie. They were
too much of a coincidence, those two. It was too slick, too
timely. They had dropped on to the stage with all the precision
of a cheap and well constructed melodrama. He went to see
the Chief Inspector about his uncertainties, and used precisely
that phrase.

"That puts it in a nut-shell," the Chief Inspector said, "A
well constructed melodrama. That's just what it is. And that's
what Kenworthy said it would be. He said there'd be an un-
bustable incrimination of Charlie Margerum. And along it
came—within the hour—in the shape and form of the poachers.
That's why I'm not worried. Everything's happening according
to the book."

"These poachers, sir—what sort of men are they?"

"Smooth operators."

"Village hoyboys, 1970's version?"

"No—smooth operators, Sergeant. You've met some on
your own patch, I take it? Young men—cheek of the devil."

"There's something out of gear, somewhere."

"I don't think there's anything out of gear, Sergeant. If you
were doing my job, in this county, none of this would surprise
you. I told you: poaching's reached the technological stage,
same as everything else. You ought to try policing a strip that
houses some of the most influential landowners in the country."

"You've got something on these chaps, have you?"

"Not this time. That's something I've got to forego in the
general interests of the case. And they know it, too—do you
think they'd have come forward otherwise? Played it cool, they
did. I could have blown my top—but why bother? I did a
couple of hours' shadow-boxing this morning that should prove
a useful investment for the future."

"You didn't think of holding them?"

"Of course not. They wouldn't have come forward if there'd
been a shred of holding evidence. If there'd been as much as
a feather in one of their boots, they'd know I'd have had them.
They got rid of all that first."

"They've still got to explain what they were doing on the
marsh that night."

"Have they? Have they, Sergeant? They know I know what
they were up to. They know I can't prove it. They also know
I don't want to, while there's a chance of putting them in as

prosecution witnesses. Two young men with curious tastes in fresh air who weren't actually breaking any laws.''

"They must be getting a fair cut—from Tennant?"

"Well—he's a master of well-constructed melodrama, too, isn't he?"

"It's too transparent. Tennant's leaning over far too eagerly.''

"It's not unheard-of for the likes of him to over-reach himself, Sergeant. What were you thinking of doing this afternoon?"

"Two of the Margerum women."

"Go to it, then. I'll have Kenworthy on to me if he thinks I've been wasting your time."

Sally Margerum was lunging a colt in a field littered with horse-jumps: leading the animal around a short circle on a long halter, pulling it up harshly, dragging savagely at its mouth— he thought—whenever it showed an inclination to go off at a tangent. It was a conflict of wills, a fundamental contest of discipline.

She waved in good-natured recognition.

"Just let this be a lesson to you. This is what happens to you when you try to measure up to a Margerum. Here, hold him a minute, will you?"

She handed him the halter, close under the mouth. It was a stocky little pony, mud-caked, with shaggy fetlocks and a rolling eye that seemed to Wright the personification of evil. Sally did something to a boot buckle, hopping about on the other leg to keep her balance. The pony pushed Wright backwards, trying to chew the pens in his pocket.

"He's looking for sugar, Sergeant."

"I usually go about loaded with the stuff. Just happen to have come without."

He tried to push the creature's head away. It side-stepped, kicked merrily with its hind legs, tried to snatch away from him. The rope slid painfully through his hand. He gripped and hauled.

"He only wants to play," Sally said.

"Tell him I'm not in the mood."

She took the halter from him.

"You don't move in horsey circles, Mr. Wright?"

"We only bring them out on special occasions—royal processions and the like."

"Actually, he's been a bit naughty—hence the defaulter's treatment."

"I promise I'll behave myself."

"Imperfect castration—that's his trouble."

"More vet's bills," Wright said, conversationally.

"Probably not. It's a job I've always wanted to tackle myself."

"I'll watch my step."

All perfectly friendly. She was hellishly attractive. But she took good care to advertise the danger signals.

"If you want to talk to Tom, he's gone to Bury St. Edmund's. To look at a new multiple seed drill."

"I think you can tell me as much as Tom can."

"You really ought to be careful, you know."

"Why?"

"The Margerums are essentially a men's family. They're apt to resent—"

"Not Tom, surely."

"Tom has a mind of his own."

They arrived at the house, and by the time he had managed the gate, and she had turned the pony into a stall, the topic was cold. He would come back to it.

She took him into the house, did a few things that he did not think needed doing—thrust a badly folded newspaper into a rack, emptied an ash-tray into a kitchen refuse bucket, threw a cat out of the door.

"I'm seldom in here in the daytime. Now, Sergeant—what can I do for you?"

And, suddenly, he did not know where to begin. He wanted to expose gently, to start chipping in depth when he found a crack. But she was not going to be easy. This girl would know when to head him off. There was going to be nothing unsubtle about it.

"Mrs. Margerum—" It sounded improbably formal, but it would help to show her she was up against an official line. "Mrs. Margerum—had it not been for your intervention, when Kenworthy and I were here last night, we might not have got anywhere."

"So you want me to unload a few more beans."

He waited.

"There are no more beans, Mr. Wright. All spilled. No more where those came from."

"Really?"

"Just what sort of revelation were you hoping for—purely out of feminine curiosity?"

"Comings and goings of the Margerum men-folk. Anything out of the normal run."

"Maurice was here this morning. Something about vesicular swine disease. We may be affected by a ban on pig movement. Tom's father came and drank a glass of light ale, just before lunch. Cursed the trades unions up hill and down dale."

"I said, out of the normal run."

"Nothing, Mr. Wright. Tom isn't involved. If I thought he was, I'd be the first to come and tell you—because I wouldn't want him to be."

"So there is something for him to be involved in?"

"I didn't say so."

"But you know there is?"

"We are talking hypothetically, Mr. Wright."

"We're not."

She adjusted the pages of a magazine along the edge of a coffee-table with slender fingers.

"I am," she said, with a smile of sweet finality. She was strong, Sally Margerum: a tough baby. She was not going to be broken by the rules of ordinary debate.

"Are you troubled much by poachers up here, Mrs. Margerum?"

"No. Because we don't breed game. There are pheasants and partridges in among the beet—but they got themselves there. Tom keeps a gun on his tractor, and if he shoots a brace, I don't throw them away. But we don't run to a hatchery. A bit further inland, where they go in for it in a big way, they've been a bit worried recently. There's something that looks like a main-line syndicate that seems to be getting a bit greedy. I believe the police are on to it. And I assume you are referring to the two gentlemen who say they saw Charlie."

"Your father-in-law mentioned them over his light ale, I presume."

"As a matter of fact, no. My brother-in-law rang up about it much earlier this morning."

"Terribly excited?"

"Terribly excited. Wouldn't you expect him to be?"

"At the prospect of seeing Charlie settled?"

She fingered the magazine askew again.

"I like Charlie, Mr. Wright. At least, I find something in him to like."

"That's what they all say—just before they put the boot in."

"He can be rather a squalid nuisance, Mr. Wright."

"Especially to the Margerums."

"Don't try to drive a wedge in, Mr. Wright. It won't work."

It was the same room in which they had been entertained last night—the dining area on a different level, the wrought iron screen, the potted greenery. But in broad daylight—there were picture windows, looking out across the farmland—it looked both smaller and cheaper.

"There's a limit to how far you'd go along with the Margerums," he said.

"And you're here to push me over the line."

"I'm here to reconnoiter."

"And I think that's most improper."

Improper. A little part of his mind began to play facetiously with the notion. She was sexually one of the most attractive women he had talked to for a long time—and she was irrepressibly frank about that aspect of herself—with the *Do Not Touch* signs equally unambiguous. Not that he'd touch, anyway. He was far too good a copper. But she might not know that. And the fact remained, he was letting his mind get just a trifle careless. He was allowing himself to become just a little too conscious of her. In a way, he'd let himself get a little frightened of her, too.

And in a moment of awareness, he switched all that off. Improper: of course it was improper, trying to bring about dissension between man and wife. If this conversation came out, and if the Margerums were in the clear, there could be all hell to pay.

Well, hell! He turned back to her, with the same face, the same casual line of reasoning, the same almost diffident gentleness—but an utterly different resolution.

"If there were a conspiracy of Margerums," he said, "and if Tom were in it, you'd want him out. Unless he was so far in it—and the whole thing was so rotten—that you knew you had to cover up for him.''

"Hypothesis again."

"Let's not play, either with words or with each other. You don't know whether there's a Margerum conspiracy or not—nor do you know the extent of Tom's involvement."

"I'm quite sure that Tom—"

"Don't be silly, Mrs. Margerum. You're not sure of anything of the sort. And that kind of formula will get you nowhere. I've heard it too many hundreds of times—from men's lips, too, but usually from women's. 'I'm quite sure'—you're not quite sure at all. You just don't bloody well know—and you'd give your ears to know. Well—I don't bloody well know, either. So shall we help each other to find out?"

She sat back, weary. Either he had not noticed how tired she was, or it had come over her suddenly.

"All right," she said. "All right. Let's try. Where do you want to begin?"

And then Wright made what Kenworthy told him afterwards was a professional mistake. He should simply have let Sally Margerum talk. Instead, he was so anxious to press her forward that he chose the questions for her to answer. And in so doing, he put blinkers on her.

"Did Cynthia Merridew come back to Candle Mere Farm on Monday night—after she had been to the Tennants?"

"I don't know."

"Was Tom called over to his father's, quite late on Monday?"

"Yes, he was."

She did not know that he was only guessing. He felt a weight shift from his shoulders. At last he had a new fact to show for a day's work.

"What did they talk about?"

"Oh—"

"Yes, Mrs. Margerum?"

"Sorry. I was going to say pig disease. Symptoms. Vaccines. Anything that came into my mind. But this is serious, isn't it?"

"Deadly."

"I don't know what they talked about. That's what troubles me. Tom's usually so open."

"He said pig disease?"

"That's right."

"So why were you suddenly so difficult to deceive?"

"I had an uneasy feeling."

"Triggered off by what?"

"Tell *me* something—"

"Within reason."

"Mr. Wright—a few minutes ago, you said we were going to help each other to get at the truth. And I know that that's all balls. But couldn't we just go through the motions? This business of Cynthia Merridew, and digging into the past, and Will Stratton and all that? Does a funny sort of safety razor come into the story somewhere? A thing in a shiny rectangular box, with a hard leather lining?"

"A Roll's Razor? Yes, it might well. Why do you ask?"

"I rode over to Candle Mere after lunch on Monday. Mavis—that's Maurice's wife—had promised me a pie, and I was taking her some drop-scones. We do that kind of thing. Well Cynthia Merridew was there. I was briefly introduced. But I'd heard her reputation. I wasn't attracted, and I didn't stay. But this razor thing was lying open on the arm of her chair."

"What were they saying? Did you hear?"

"It was one of those occasions when you're acutely aware that your arrival has dried a conversation up."

"But something must have been said to make you connect the razor with Will Stratton—"

"Yes, that's true. Just as I was opening the door, Miss Merridew was saying the words "steel-framed spectacles.""

"Ah!"

Sally Margerum narrowed her eyes.

"Mr. Wright—I do believe you don't know what I am talking about. Am I one up on you, for a change? This is where I might try a spot of trade—"

Wright shook his head.

"Mrs. Margerum—you know damned well there's no trade. Close season."

"How right you are! Sorry. I thought the steel-framed spectacles were everybody's property—part and parcel of the Stratton legend. Maybe it's something that's stayed in the family."

"Like a lot of things."

She ignored this.

"May I say that I don't know much about Will Stratton. Tom doesn't care for the subject. I've never dared discuss it with Charlie, and it's anathema within ear-shot of my father-in-law. But Tom did once mention that the only thing that was ever found of him was this pair of spectacles. I think he used them only for reading, and they were an extremely ugly pair— First World War army issue, I think. They were found by a hired hand, ploughing a field."

"Which field?"

"I don't know. I should ask Tom or Maurice, rather than their father."

"And when was this?"

"During the war—the second one—is that a useful contribution of beans?"

"Any more in the bushel?"

"No, that's it, Mr. Wright. Precious little—"

"It's enough to have had you worrying about Tom."

"Not about him—for him."

"Does that distinction matter much?"

"If I could do anything to help."

"You can."

"What's that?"

There was no doubting her eagerness.

"Tell Tom to come and see us—and talk!"

"You make it sound so easy."

"We shall have to try, if you don't.

She showed him to the door, and as she closed it behind him, he heard her relief, thinking him already out of hearing.

"Whew!" she said.

A tough baby: she sounded as if she were congratulating herself on getting away with something.

·14·

CROSSING THE FIELDS by the short cut from Drove Farm to Candle Mere, Wright was able to survey the original Franklin property as it had appeared to Joe Margerum from over the fence, when Maud and Will were wintering together. He must have seethed at the sight of the couple, dots against the static landscape. Day after day, he must have watched Will at work, have seen the curl of smoke from the farm-house chimney, and have known that the pair were closeted together in warmth and solitude.

But the face of the countryside was changing. Tom Margerum, the innovator, had grubbed up miles of his internal hedgerows. A team of outside contractors was working today, felling a copse of diseased elms. Wright passed an orchard where Will and Maud had tended a flock of free-range hens. Now there was the low hum of ventilator motors from a row of long, gray battery sheds.

He tried to pick out Will's bunk-house, and thought he spotted it—a single-story hut of creosoted weather-board, with the iron pipe of a stove chimney. But it was difficult to know for certain: there had been an accretion of new structures: Dutch barns on concrete foundations, and fuel tanks to feed the mechanization that had been introduced all over the place.

Then he had the almost supernatural feeling that he was not alone in the spot. A pair of eyes was watching him; he stopped, and looked all around, but saw no one. And yet the certainty was so strong that after a few yards he pulled himself up short again, even left the path to go and look over a wall. Again, nobody.

He negotiated the fastening of the gate that let him into the main yard of Candle Mere. And then he saw the figure, gray and absolutely motionless, watching him from the doorway of a derelict sty: Kenworthy.

So what was the old sod up to now? How long since he'd doubled back from Lynn, having been nowhere near London at all?

Kenworthy raised a hand and held his finger against his lips. Wright passed on and tried to put himself into the right frame of mind for Mavis Margerum. What was he going to make of the pudding?

Once inside the house, he succeeded in isolating her for less than two minutes. Maurice was away for the afternoon—looking at another man's method of fodder-storage in a distant part of the county. But before Wright had finished putting his first question, she was calling her father-in-law from his afternoon rest to come and be present. Wright let it go—at least for the time being—telling himself that there was little he could hope to do with her. He could only play with the pair of them and hope for the satisfaction of springing a verbal trap.

Joe Margerum came in looking decidedly puffy about the eyes. Was this the man who had ridden up on Christmas morning with the ivory-handled crop and cavalry boots?

"A Roll's Razor?" Wright asked. "What was it Cynthia Merridew was saying about a Roll's Razor?"

"There was something," Mavis said. "I do seem to remember something—"

She bounced the question off toward her father-in-law.

"She did say something about a razor, didn't she, Dad?"

Wright welcomed the opportunity to shorten his temper.

"You may have time for amateur dramatics, but I haven't. She had it on display on the arm of that chair."

They would know that this came from Sally, but this was all to the good. It could be useful for them to be wondering how much else Sally might have overheard.

"She was showing it to us," Margerum said.

"Clearly. Why?"

Margerum teetered on the brink of the distasteful.

"She claimed that it had belonged to Stratton."

"And had it?"

Joe Margerum erupted.

"I neither know nor care. What is there between one Roll's

Razor and another? They were very much in vogue at one time. As far as I'm concerned, one is the twin of the next.''

Wright prolonged the discomfort.

''At least, we are making better progress than we did yesterday. We now seem generally agreed on a connection between Miss Merridew and Will Stratton. How had this thing come into her possession?''

''She didn't say.''

''Then why did she bring the subject up at all?''

''You know what she was like, Sergeant Wright. At least, you don't, but you should be building up a rough idea, by now. Always dabbling in things that didn't concern her—always messing about with some silly little corner of the past.''

Wright looked at Mavis. It was difficult to tell what was going on behind those coarse, bucolic features. She was not intelligent, and behind her dark, lifeless eyes was the bucolic's fear of an intelligent world. If he was prepared to leave her out of the conversation, she was content to stay out of it.

''And what was it that interested her in this particular corner?''

''How would I know?''

''I was under the impression that that was what she came here to tell you.''

''It was impossible to know what she was talking about, half the time.''

''About a pair of steel-framed spectacles, for example?''

''Since you seem to know so much—''

''I need to know more.''

''For God's sake, Sergeant—why don't you go off and deal with the things that matter?''

''Steel-framed spectacles, Mr. Margerum—''

''Picked up thirty years ago, twenty years after they had been dropped.''

Wright smiled to annoy him.

''You obviously believe in round figures. Dropped in 1926 and picked up in—when was it?—1942?''

''And that is supposed to prove something? All this has nothing to do with Miss Merridew.''

''Then why did she come here to talk about it?''

He swung toward the woman.

''Steel-framed spectacles, Mrs. Margerum—''

Joe Margerum tried to answer for her.

"I think she was thinking of writing—"

"I'm asking *her*, Mr. Margerum—"

Mavis Margerum moistened her lips.

"That's it: she was going to turn it into a story."

"Tell me about these spectacles."

"They were found on the edge of the five-acre. They are supposed to have belonged to Will Stratton."

"And where does the Roll's Razor come into the story? Where was that found?"

"She didn't say. She *wouldn't* say."

Margerum interrupted.

"She insisted on making a mystery of it. I don't believe, anyway, that it was the same razor."

"The same razor as what?"

Cornered, Margerum had to reply.

"It had been a present. A present from my wife to Stratton before I really knew her."

"A birthday present?"

"A Christmas present."

The resurrection of the incident was wholly distasteful to him.

"Did you ever give her a Christmas present at that period of her life, Mr. Margerum? A marquetry box, for example, with a stretch of coast-line on the lid, a sea-gull and a leaning groyne?"

Margerum was now desperately puzzled. Even Cynthia Merridew, who had not seen the diary, had not mentioned the box. Wright decided on quick-fire mystification.

"I want to see that box, Margerum."

"I doubt whether it is still in the house."

"I believe you could put your fingers on it in two seconds."

"It is wholly irrelevant. And your impertinence—"

"Please go and get it, Mr. Margerum—"

Margerum was now on his feet.

"I do not know what you are talking about. I do not know why you have to spend every moment of your working day prying into these distressing privacies."

The tension of the moment was so great that they did not hear the door open. A quiet voice cut in on them.

"Not co-operating, Margerum?"

Margerum wheeled round, seemed unable at first to take in Kenworthy's presence.

"You don't have to do as my Sergeant asks. He can always sit with you while I go and get a warrant. It will be given for the asking."

Margerum stood for a moment as if determined to refuse. Then, with a convulsive twitch of his shoulders, he turned on his heel and left the room. Maurice's wife was left unprotected, with one detective in front of her, and one behind. Kenworthy reverted to his soft-tongued approach.

"It must be very bewildering, Mrs. Margerum, to find yourself overtaken like this by family history with which you have no connection."

"I shall thank God when this has all blown over."

"What makes you think it's going to blow over?"

Kenworthy's confidence seemed to startle her.

"*Is* it going to blow over, Mrs. Margerum?"

"I should hope so."

"Mrs. Margerum—a woman has been killed."

"Not for any of the reasons that you are wasting your time on."

"For what reasons, then?"

The woman then took shameless refuge behind her stupidity. She set her jaw, and looked Kenworthy in the eye, and refused to answer. And for the moment she was saved by the arrival of her father-in-law back in the room. He was carrying the box, and he placed it on the table, first emptying its contents on to a sheet of newspaper.

"There's nothing there that need interest you. But I have touched nothing; you cannot accuse me of interfering."

There were one or two rings, a wrist-watch without a strap, a few old letters, a seaside postcard. Wright handled the box. It was about the size he had expected, presentably amateurish in its execution, but much spoiled in its appearance by deterioration of the varnish.

"And you made this yourself?"

"I did. And what good has the sight of it done you?"

"It helps me to reconstruct things, Mr. Margerum."

Kenworthy came across, and picked the box up.

"A whole life," he said, "controlled and shaped by hatred."

"I have never hated any man."

"Not Will Stratton?"

"I didn't have to. Stratton ran away."

"And why do you think he ran away—at the moment when things were just starting to break even with him?"

"Fear of responsibility. Fear of being overtaken by routines. Boredom after conquest. The traditional pattern of the seducer. Stratton saw the shape of things to come. What future was there for him here? They spent the whole of their time quarreling. I heard them myself—there was no need even to approach the house."

"And you've closed your mind to any other possible interpretation?"

"What other possible interpretation is there, Superintendent?"

"That the couple had in fact just solved the problem of how to live together—perhaps not conventionally, but at any rate in peace. That they had even got as far as short-listing places to which they might go."

"He had already run away from one woman and child."

"The circumstances were not comparable."

"You are talking as Miss Merridew talked. I presume she left behind some sort of memorandum, which you have found."

"And which you would dearly love to see," Kenworthy said.

The woman was now looking steadily at her father-in-law. If such a document indeed existed as Margerum had in mind, it would undoubtedly have accused him uncompromisingly of murder.

"Miss Merridew was mad," he said at last. "I don't think there would be any dissentient from that."

"Mr. Margerum, I have reason to believe that fairly late on Monday evening, after having coffee with your daughter and son-in-law in their bungalow, Miss Merridew returned here."

Margerum stared at him for a second. Mavis seemed to raise both arms at once, then let them fall again.

"I will be honest with you," Margerum said. "We were expecting her. She said when she left us in the afternoon, she would be back."

"You could have saved us a lot of trouble by telling us that yesterday."

"I behaved foolishly."

"If you think that that is a disarming admission, Mr. Margerum, I hasten to disillusion you. And I think it's time we started getting some of this on paper. Sergeant Wright—"

So Kenworthy left him with the laborious task of drawing up the statements. As he let himself out of the room, the Superintendent repeated his gesture of holding his finger to his lips. He did not say where he was going, or when Wright would see him again.

Wright waited until all the sheets were signed before he asked why Tom had been called over from the other farm, late on the Monday night. Margerum repeated—and Mavis confirmed—the story about swine disease.

So there was all the bother about making separate additional statements, with which the pair complied irritably. Wright did not try to budge them from the story. It might be very useful, later, to have the makings of a formal retraction to cajole from them.

·15·

IT WAS A slow, even twilight, that seemed to draw the world into itself. Everything was still—as if the whole country-side was in suspense, the only signs of life a showing of smoke from the chimneys of the village. And even that had only risen a few feet and seemed caught in the universal silence, hanging motionless over the red pantile roofs. About the farm, some laborer had been carting silage. There was something almost homely and comforting about the mordant, cheesey smell.

It was going to be a cold night. Already there was a sparkle of frost on hard surfaces. Last autumn's leaves were brittle underfoot.

Spend as much time as he could with Charlie, Kenworthy had said. Wright found the prospect a relief as if, after a day of unsympathetic company, he were heading for the presence of someone whose sense of values he did not question.

He crossed the yard between the two farms, picking his way along the mucky drive of Marsh Hall. The front of the house was deserted and inert: some of the windows uncurtained, others hung with heavy velvet that had not been taken down for years. He went around to the back: there was not a sign of life. Perhaps Charlie was still out: though as he was alone in a small boat, it hardly seemed likely that he would delay his return after nightfall. A knock on the back door brought no response other than a flurry of farm-yard poultry. Wright looked in desultory fashion around the yard. Uneven stone steps, their rails long since broken away, led up to the end wall of a granary; a rat peeped out from the timber-pile that contained all that remained of the cock-pit; a man-size shrimping-net was leaning against a wall.

Then Wright heard an internal combustion engine in low

gear—an engine in bad condition, blowing out through a perforated exhaust, and the rattle of a loose bracket. Charlie came in sight, towing his dinghy on a two-wheeled trailer. He looked as pleased to see Wright as Wright was to see him. It might have been a reunion of old friends.

"Had to go back and fetch her up," Charlie said. "Dunno what's happened to her. Thwart cracked across, and a timber stove in. Stove out, rather. The damage was done from inside. I've been baling like a lunatic all day."

"Do you carry many heavy loads in her?"

"Never. Forty pound tope, last October."

"When were you last out in her?"

"Sunday morning."

"You don't usually bring her back up here?"

"Moored to a stake, side of the Leam. Anybody borrowed her, they'd have to bring her back, wouldn't they? Not that there's ever anybody about."

His accent was much broader than the rest of his family, as if even in speech he stood apart from them.

"You weren't out Tuesday night?"

"So help me, no. Couldn't have seen my own bows."

He left the van parked where he had stopped, askew against a wall.

"Your boat was out," Wright told him. "And your van. You were seen."

"I been seen often in places where I ain't been."

"Seriously, though."

"Indoors from cockshut time. Who reckons to have seen me?"

"Poachers—professionals."

"Professionals?"

Charlie's surprise seemed spontaneous. He drew from his pocket a key that looked as if it belonged to a medieval church, and let them into the house.

"Much of a bag for professionals hereabouts?" Wright asked him.

"I wouldn't have said so. A bit further inland—"

"Not duck on the marshes?"

"I wouldn't see a fortune in duck, Mr. Wright."

"Not in the London markets?"

"I don't know what sells in the London markets."

"Well, let's say, they let it be thought they were poachers," Wright said.

The house was cold. Charlie had appeared to have left it that morning with no source of heating at all. But he had sticks, coal and newspapers ready laid out, and set to work at once on the grate of his large room. There seemed to be something about the poachers that troubled him more than anything had troubled him last night. He came back quickly to the subject.

"Those two who reckon they saw me—local men? What are they called?"

Wright told him their names. They meant nothing to him.

"And they saw me?"

"So they say. And your van. And your boat."

"But how do they know me? I don't know them. Though somebody had my boat. Somebody bust it up."

"Not surprising. It wasn't built for carrying scaffolds about."

"They've got a bloody nerve," Charlie said.

"What surprises you about it? You've known all along that your scaffold was used. If they'd transported it in any other way, they'd have had to use the road. And they'd have had a parking problem."

"I can see that."

Charlie was still upset about something. He blew on a sparking stick, and his nest of kindling caught flame with a sudden splutter.

"What's eating you, Charlie?"

"It's just that—this makes it all seem so bloody real—doesn't it?"

"It hasn't seemed real to you up to now?"

"It has, and it hasn't. God damn it, I'm talking twaddle. What am I trying to say?"

"I think I know, Charlie."

"Somebody's trying to get me," Charlie said.

"And who do you think that might be?"

Charlie played vacantly with coal on the fire. He was trying to work it out—and finding no satisfaction. Was this because he was reluctant to settle on any individual? Was he so basically naive that he found it hard to believe that anyone would try to frame him? Suddenly, he seemed to push the enigma clean out of his mind. He beat his hands together and stood up from his haunches.

"All I can offer you for supper is a few dabs. Caught practically sod all today. Spent most of my time baling. Like to find yourself something to read while I go and gut them?"

"I'd rather come and watch the chef at work."

The kitchen was ice-box cold. Its equipment was reminiscent of a folk-museum: a pump over the edge of a chipped stone sink, a row of pots and steamers a century old, a Calor gas cooker that must have been a pioneer model. It was difficult to tell whether the place was clean or not: the worn chopping-board, the pitted brick floor and the irregular cup-hooks screwed into the plaster did not lend themselves to gleam and sparkle. But the roller-towel on the door was fresh though torn, and a tea-cloth hanging over a pan-handle was more or less white. The place was orderly. Nothing was lying about: Charlie brought out a knife tapered down by much sharpening and dealt deftly with the fish. He melted dripping in a pan.

"Never thought of getting married?" Wright asked.

"Often."

"Nothing ever came of it?"

"Never got out of the thinking stage. I've got yesterday's mashed potato we can fry up. I often do that. Tin of peas. Bread and cheese. That do you?"

They carried the food back to the living-room and ate surrounded by Charlie's books. He was not long in coming back to his principal hurt.

"Somebody's trying to frame me."

"You must have known that, Charlie, ever since he borrowed your drop."

"I've known it, Mr. Wright—I've only just realized it. Do you understand?"

"I think so. But what's brought it home to you like this?"

"Bringing in outsiders to swear the tale. I've met London poachers. I know what sort of men they are."

"Don't go too fast, Charlie. There's no basis for saying that they were brought in. They may just happen to have been there."

"But I wasn't."

"No. And they didn't see you. No man could have been sure of another, at that distance, on a night like that. But they did see your van, they did see your boat, they did see your Dutchman's bridge, and they did see a bundle that was surely Cynthia Merridew.''

Charlie chewed thoughtfully. The fish was marvelously fresh. It had been fried in tasty fat. The potatoes had come up a golden brown.

''So if these two poachers—admitting what they were up to—came forward on their own accord—''

There was no doubting Charlie's intelligence. He had crossed a large gap quickly.

''They didn't come forward of their own accord.''

''Oh? Then somebody—''

Wright hesitated. He did not want to implicate Tennant at this stage. Charlie might lose his head and start a process of his own. On the other hand, he could not afford to lose Charlie's confidence. He changed the angle quickly.

''In any case, Charlie—it isn't new for you to be framed, is it?''

''I don't follow you, Mr. Wright.''

''I was thinking of the time you went to prison.''

''I wasn't framed then, Mr. Wright.''

''I'll take your word for that. You ought to know. But didn't you even wonder?''

''No.''

Wright looked at him and wondered how he had suffered during his sentence—this eccentric, contemplative, slow-spoken man, with his sense of philosophical nobility behind the rough appearance. Or perhaps, before some point of change, he had been nothing but a tearaway.

''You were saying, Mr. Wright, about these poachers—''

''Do you mind if we leave that for a moment, Charlie? We'll come back to it later. I'd like, if you'll forgive my stirring the memory, to ask something else about that jail sentence.''

''It doesn't trouble me, Mr. Wright.''

''It must have upset your mother terribly. What was her attitude to Joe Margerum concerning it?''

''I can't remember that there was anything special. There was always—''

''Yes, Charlie?''

''There was always a bit of difficulty with Joe Margerum, if he thought she was coming over here too often. I mean, he didn't ever try to stop her. That's something she wouldn't have stood for. But he didn't like it. So she didn't draw his attention to it unnecessarily.''

''But she stood for it when you took the blame for all of them.''

''I wouldn't have got less than six months if they'd all come to Norwich with me. Not that I'm saying they were guilty of anything. But I know what you're getting at, Mr. Wright. And you're wrong. I wasn't framed by Joe and Maurice—then or now.''

''You seem pretty sure.''

''They're not that sort of people, Mr. Wright.''

''You're being very charitable, Charlie.''

''They don't like me. I'm not a very likeable sort of fellow, in their book. But that's a very different thing. You meet too many criminals in your job—''

''Charlie—this murder wasn't the work of a criminal—not in the professional sense.''

''You mean, not like the poachers.''

''You keep leading me back to them, Charlie.''

''What do you expect? They're the ones who could do for me, if you cared to listen to them. I want to know—''

''Charlie—''

''Oh, I know, Mr. Wright—you don't want to tell me. Can't blame you for that, I suppose. I know which way your mind is working.''

His coolness and his consistent lack of malice were amazing.

''You've got your job to do, Mr. Wright. You must choose your own way of doing it. I'd like to help. But if you don't want me to ask awkward questions, I shall have to stay in ignorance of the answers.''

How true was the image? Dark jowls, dark eyes, negligent of his appearance, wild man of the past, might he suddenly break out, savage and uncontrolled? Was the disarming candor only a facade? What would be the change in the picture, if Charlie could be made to lose his temper?

''You'd like to know who brought the poachers forward, Charlie—''

''Does that surprise you?''

''But you know already, don't you?''

''How can I, Mr. Wright? I've been lying off the estuary

all day. But I shall find out tomorrow, as soon as I go out. That'll be all over the village.''

"But you don't need to go to the village, do you, Charlie? You know already, without being told, because you know who it *would* be—''

Charlie shook his head with a gentle laugh and the softest of tones.

"I wouldn't like to make any mistake. We're both trying to make each other say a man's name, Mr. Wright—isn't that what we're doing? And neither of us will. Have a piece of cheese.''

"Thank you. Let's change the subject. Tell me what you think about Major Tennant.''

"He's clever, Mr. Wright, very clever. Though I haven't read any of his books. Not right through, that is.''

"I'm surprised, you know, that the thought of having you as a neighbor wasn't enough to keep him out of the county.''

Charlie chuckled.

"I know nothing of his disfavor, Mr. Wright.''

"Nor even suspect anything, I suppose? All right. I won't press you. But tell me this: have you ever had anything to do with him at all? I mean, other than starchy little family meetings?''

"We both like to take a gun out on the marshes.''

"Together often?''

"Not often.''

"When was the last time?''

"I shall have to look that up—''

To Wright's surprise, Charlie went to a shelf just before floor level and brought out a foolscap manuscript book. He turned back page after page of Vere Foster copybook handwriting.

"This is *my* diary, Mr. Wright—thirty years of it. And no need to keep this locked up. There's nothing here that the next man mustn't read.''

"What on earth do you find to write about?''

"Thoughts, mostly—ah, here we are: November 17th. Six brace of mallard. Two of wigeon. Two of sheld-duck. One smew. Observed gadwall, east-north-east of Hickling's—probably a visitor—''

"Do you mean to say you write something every day?''

"Most days. Some days more happens than others.''

"Like my life, too. And what sort of thing did you put, say, the day Cynthia Merridew came to the cock-fight?"

Charlie waved about with his forefinger, then lighted on the spine of the right volume.

"Mind you, you won't find a word about cock-fighting there. *Northern Lights*, I always used to call it."

"You use a lot of code-names like that?"

"That would be telling, Mr. Wright. A man's entitled to his secrets—and I haven't committed a crime against the laws of the land for eighteen years. And what is a crime, Mr. Wright? How would you define the word?"

"In my line of country, it's any infringement of the laws laid down by parliamentary government."

"Myself, I put it rather differently."

"I'm sure you do. But a one-man morality can be dangerous, Charlie. One man can make mistakes. And one man sometimes has to work with others."

"I've done very little of that in my time."

"Have you done much in company with Major Tennant?"

"I've put him in the way of a bit of duck-shooting."

"And what's that a code-name for?"

Charlie grinned happily.

"Ever since I met you, Mr. Wright, I've been watching the working of your mind. You're one of the most suspicious men I've ever met."

"I consider that praise—professionally speaking."

"But you're fair with it, if I may say so. If every policeman was as fair as you seem to be."

Again Wright had the impression of his first meeting with the man—that he was the one who was truly in command of the situation. His eccentricity was a shelter behind which he could get away with anything. And if this was neither fallacy nor accident, then he was a very astute operator indeed—and a very dangerous one. Wright headed him down a different track.

"Who was the bearded gentleman with whom Miss Merridew had an appointment Monday lunch-time?"

"That would be old Dr. Wilshaw from the other side of Spalding."

The answer was so prompt and so confident that Wright wanted to laugh.

"Why the hell didn't we ask you that before?"

"Not a medical doctor. Doctor of history, or some such thing. She told me she was going to meet him."

"You know the man, do you?"

"She brought him here once, years ago. And he'd made some discovery out Fosdyke way he was going to tell her about—"

Wright was making notes.

"Dr. Wilshaw, Spalding area, academic—"

"He's harmless," Charlie said, reaching heights of the unintentionally comic.

"Is he a man who's had much to do with Mawson's Drove?"

"Hardly at all."

"Not known locally?"

"I'd say unknown locally."

"But she brought him here once?"

"To see Luyk's scaffold, when I first made it."

"What was her relationship with him?"

"I don't know that there was one."

"Now come on, Charlie. If two people have lunch together, that's a relationship."

"I'd say it was the same relationship she had with people all over the country who could tell her little bits of local history—university professors and the like."

"And what sort of new discovery was it at Fosdyke?"

"There was a story there that a laborer had been killed by one of the early threshing engines. His arm got caught up, and he bled to death before they could get him out. Blood spurting out on the corn like it was gushing from a pump. That was the time of the Captain Swing riots. Machinery wasn't all that popular."

"Sounds like the sort of tale that would appeal to her."

"Dr. Wilshaw reckoned he had found the original machine, stowed away in the back of a barn."

Wright could not resist a shaft of cynicism.

"I suppose she wanted to chance her own arm in the works."

But Charlie did not like the remark.

"Don't poke fun at her, Mr. Wright. And don't get the wrong idea about that hanging—the one we photographed. I know what she was trying to do. I was there. I saw her face—I took the picture; she showed me how to work the camera. A moment of truth, she called it.''

''She found her moment of truth all right, Charlie—or somebody found it for her. Only I don't think she had much time to savor it when it finally happened.''

There was then a moment of silence, each man thinking in his own way of the woman's last moments.

''I tell you, Mr. Wright—I know what she was trying to find. I know what she was trying to understand. She used to say that death was the biggest thing in life. It haunted us from the moment we were big enough to hear about it. It certainly haunted her—she had to know what it was going to feel like.''

''Self-torture.''

''More than that—self-education, she said. She said experience was the only source of knowledge.''

''Charlie—can I ask you a very personal question?''

''Ask me anything you like, Mr. Wright.''

''Did you ever have sex with Cynthia Merridew?''

''I never had sex with anybody, Mr. Wright.''

''And Cynthia Merridew?''

''She wanted to have sex with me that night—I thought Mr. Kenworthy understood that, the way he spoke—''

''He did. But what about Cynthia Merridew and other men?''

''I'm not in a position to know, Mr. Wright.''

''But if you did, would you feel just a little jealous?''

Charlie considered his answer. Loose wire rattled against the window-pane, as it had last night.

''Yes, Mr. Wright, I would. I know, because I've wondered about that. And I know that now. And that's what our relationship was. I've known her thirty years, and I suppose over that time I've seen her about thirty times. I don't have sex with women, Mr. Wright. I've wanted it, same as the next man, but there are hindrances. I get sort of disgusted. Do you know what I mean?''

''I think so.''

''Cynthia Merridew—she identified herself with a fighting-cock that had its guts torn out, and it made her sort of drunk. It was a bloody good fight, that was. I never saw the likes of it. And when that bird died, it gave in like it was happy to be finished. I don't know whether I'm making myself plain.''

''Plain enough, Charlie.''

"Well, if there was ever a man alive who could have made her as happy as that dying fowl did, I wouldn't like to have done her out of the chance of it. But I wish it could have been me. I still wish it could have been me. Does that answer your question, Sergeant?"

It did. But it also reminded Wright how far all this was from a report that could go forward. You had to get to know your people, that was axiomatic. But you could let yourself get fascinated—and lost.

The wire clapped against the pane again. A burning coal fell forward against the bars. Wright listened intently—he thought he heard a car engine running outside. It was not the first time he had strained his ears in this house. Faintly, he was sure he could hear men's voices. Then Charlie kicked up a racket with poker and tongs.

"Quiet a minute, Charlie! I think we have visitors!"

They went together to the door, saw even before they opened it that the yard was flooded with light: headlamps, engines running, portable flood-lamps on stands, policemen with dogs, photographers. There were at least half a dozen vehicles, including a van that could carry a patrol of thirty men.

"I have a warrant to search these premises, Margerum."

Kenworthy waved a piece of paper under Charlie's nose.

"Bring him with us, Sergeant Wright. I want him to be watching when we find what we're going to find."

·16·

IT WAS AN untidy operation. The members of the team knew their jobs, but they had not worked together before. They were unfamiliar with the geography of the yard. Someone reversed a patrol car just as someone else was trying to read a document in its beams. The dog-handler got in the way of a photographer carrying heavy equipment.

"Chief Inspector—get hold of them, will you? How much of this racket was audible in the house, Sergeant?"

"Barely heard it, sir. Charlie didn't hear it at all."

"As I thought. Margerum, show us exactly where that scaffold of yours was lying."

They went over to the wood-pile. Charlie indicated an area. They could see where the hard edges of the timber had dug into the earth. The ground was frozen hard, a worm's tunnel clearly visible in torch-light. Kenworthy looked around.

"Up there!"

He pointed to the stone steps, against the outside wall of the granary. The Chief Inspector had now lined up his minions into a disciplined parade and was addressing them from a clipped mill-board. But there was still a self-appointed committee on Kenworthy's heels. He wheeled on them.

"One photographer, one fingerprints, Sergeant Wright and Margerum. The rest of you go and sit in the cars you came in."

He led the way up the worn and broken steps.

"If you wanted to bring someone up here, Shiner, who wasn't all that anxious to come, on a cold and clammy night—"

"I'd tell her a tale, sir, the sort of thing I knew she'd like to hear, with the promise of a gruesome relic on the other side of that door."

"Is that how you did it, then, Charlie?"

Charlie grunted a mixture of surprise and dismay.

"You and who else was it, Charlie? It took two of you, that's for sure. Even Pierrepoint had an assistant."

They had reached the platform at the top. It had once had a rail. Kenworthy shone his torch on a gap between the bricks, where a beam had once protruded to form the arm of a hoist.

"When did that disappear, Charlie?"

"Rotted away before I ever took the farm."

"Pity. It would have made a good gibbet."

He tried the door, but could not make it budge. Charlie stepped forward and kicked it with the side of his foot.

"Sticks a bit, that's all."

Inside was a spacious granary, untidy, but not overcrowded, swept but not scrubbed. There were pieces of archaic equipment hanging from the walls, mostly broken; the handle of a flail, a wooden yoke for carrying buckets, bits of old harness. There was a smell of saddle-soap, fish-meal and chaff.

Kenworthy went straight to a trap in the floor, and pulled it up by its iron ring.

"Opens the wrong way. What did you do? Make her jump— or give her a push?"

They looked down into a double stable. The hatch opened directly over the manger, so that fodder could be lowered from above. But it was a long time since horses had been stalled there. An outboard motor was lying in the rack, and the bows of a boat were visible—fiberglass, contemporary in its lines, little short of flashy.

Kenworthy looked up at block and tackle, grouted into a rafter over the hole.

"When did you last use that, Charlie?"

"Before the war."

"There's fresh oil on it—well, it's gathered a couple of day's rust. Try it for dabs. I doubt whether there'll be any."

Then he looked closely at the surrounding floor and walls, knelt and peered over the edge, grunting eventually with satisfaction at something he saw.

"I'd like a look around below."

"I'll have to go get the key."

"Go with him, Shiner."

This gave Charlie, as Wright had expected, an embarrassing chance to unburden himself.

"Mr. Kenworthy's talking now as if he thought I did it."

And Wright knew better than to relieve the tension that Kenworthy had not created accidentally.

"Kenworthy's been away all day. I don't know yet what he's come up with."

"Not you, too, Mr. Wright?"

The key was in a drawer. It was a Yale, and it looked new.

"I'll just say one thing to you, Charlie—if you've got anything on your mind, anything at all you haven't told us yet— let's be having it."

"There's nothing, Mr. Wright—have a word with him for me—"

"If I'm any judge of form, you'll be having a word with him yourself before long."

The group was gathered around the stable door, none of them talking. Kenworthy was impatient to get in. The torchlights caught the steam of their breath on the frosty air.

They were staggered at the sight of the boat. It was mint new, had a slick covered cock-pit, looked extraordinarily powerful.

"No wonder you've had a new lock fitted," Kenworthy said.

But he paid no more attention to it. He went straight to the area under the trap-door, stretching out his arms to keep the others from crowding either him or the evidence.

He looked for things one at a time: first the scraped whitewash, where her heels had kicked the wall.

"That's where she did her dance. They didn't drop her far enough. That's why her neck wasn't broken. They ought to have borrowed the Home Office tables. Measure it, Shiner."

And when Wright had finished, Kenworthy compared the figures with some he had in a notebook.

"Fits in with the length of rope on the body. Probably left it on between the two operations."

He examined a smear on the wall, took a scraping for the laboratory.

"Blood. Grazed knee. Now for it."

He hoisted himself on to the manger, got his foot on to the upper rail.

"Watch it, sir—that wall bracket—"

Kenworthy took no notice. Leaning on the wall with one shoulder, his instep jammed against the rail, he reached up to the edge of the gap.

"Stand by to receive evidence, Sergeant."

Shreds of material of two kinds: a wisp of what looked like synthetic fur, less than a square centimeter of brownish cloth, caught against a protruding nail-head. They came from opposite sides of the trap. Cynthia Merridew had been hauled up afterward, pulled as she swung, no attempt at gentleness.

Charlie, surely, would have used the key—dropped her to the floor and come down to collect. This party had done it the hard way.

Kenworthy stepped back with his shoulder against the boat.

"How much fuel does she carry?"

"Hundred gallons."

"Give H.M. Customs cutter a run for its money in that."

"Never tried, Mr. Kenworthy."

"There's always tomorrow."

They came out into the yard again. The parade had fallen out, and the men were standing about in quiet knots. There was a universal quickening of limbs when Kenworthy emerged—but he paid no attention to it.

"That yours?"

He went to Charlie's van, parked as it was with the trailer and dinghy behind it.

"Yes, Mr. Kenworthy."

"I want you to drive us down to the Leam—just the Sergeant and me."

"It will be easier without the trailer."

"We shall need it. We're going to use the boat."

Kenworthy sat in the passenger seat. Charlie drove reasonably, but with no great regard for his springs. Wright crouched in the back, almost choked by the smell of fish, sheep and manure. The windscreen quickly misted over, and an icy draft came up from the floor.

"How far, Mr. Kenworthy?"

"You know."

The headlamps picked up an edge of dike. There was a sharp turn over a very narrow bridge. A rabbit ran in front of them,

raced straight ahead of them for several yards, hadn't the sense
to turn aside.

"I've got two moorings, Mr. Kenworthy."

"The one you used on Tuesday night."

"I wasn't here on Tuesday night."

"The one you think was used on Tuesday."

Charlie did not answer, but put his right hand down. The
wheels of the trailer rattled over a stone.

"Why've you chosen this one?"

"There's a bit of a landing-stage. It would have been easier,
with a body to handle."

"Somebody who knew the locality well."

"It looks that way, doesn't it? Mr. Kenworthy, one minute
you talk as if you think I did it, the next minute it's someone
else."

"That's about the way of it, Charlie. One minute I think
one thing—"

"Here we are, then."

It was a barren spot on the edge of the narrow water-course.
The grass was short, and already white with rime. Kenworthy
looked about them, found nothing. Away across a field, a torch
was switched on and off. He had posted someone where the
poachers claimed to have been.

"Let's get the boat out. Is it deep enough?"

The tide was on the ebb. A foot or so of mud showed above
the water-line.

"She draws less than two feet—but she's letting in a lot of
water, Mr. Kenworthy—"

"Shiner's a dab-hand with a baler."

Kenworthy stood by while Charlie and Wright manhandled
the dinghy.

"Feasible up to now, but I wish we'd brought the scaffold.
I'd like to have seen how it handled."

"They smashed my thwart with it, Mr. Kenworthy."

Charlie took the oars. Water splashed. The baler was an old
Mackintosh's sweet tin. Charlie pulled leisurely, untroubled
by his load and unworried by their slow progress. In places the
reeds on either side rose above their heads—but these at least
did provide a modicum of shelter. In the open spaces the east-
erly wind made nonsense of the clothes they were wearing.

"I'm thinking, Mr. Kenworthy."

"I'd hoped you might."

"If I'd been doing this, I wouldn't have rowed right up to the culvert."

"Why not?"

"There's only one reason to come this way, and that's so as not to be seen from the road. But I'd have gone no further than the next bend."

"Can you moor there?"

"I'd beach her bows."

"Do that, then."

As they stepped on to the bank, it was Kenworthy this time who signaled with a torch. The reply came in a pinpoint of light, two hundred yards away.

"You could well be right, Charlie."

They walked together to the culvert. The brown water swirled against the brick-work. There was a tang of brine, rotting seaweed, damp stone.

"Thank you, Charlie. You can go home now. The way you came."

"Yes, Mr. Kenworthy. Does that mean—?"

"It means nothing, Charlie. Nothing means anything."

Wright and Kenworthy crossed the old sea-wall and slogged over the field.

"Inspector," Kenworthy said.

"I beg your pardon."

"I haven't been to London, Shiner. Only to King's Lynn. Sid Heather brought Will Stratton down—and one or two other bits of things. And he told me you're an Inspector. There's an Establishment Order in the pipe-line. You're going to P Division."

Wright could not think of anything to say.

"End of a beautiful relationship, Shiner."

"I hope not, sir."

"We shan't be seeing much more of each other. People always hope so, but they never do. And there's another thing, Shiner: do you remember once when I did threaten to break off the friendship—unilaterally?"

"Actually, sir, it's happened more than once."

"Once in particular, when I meant it—or thought I did— for a whole hour or more. When you lost a man—"

"Albert Boardman."

"I've never been so angry with any man in my life, as I was with you that afternoon, Shiner."

"I remember sir. But—"

"No buts, Shiner. I'm trying to lead up to something."

They had reached the road. Kenworthy was silent for several paces.

"I lost a man, this morning, Shiner."

"Will Stratton?"

It crossed Wright's mind that it might be a hoax. He had never been firmly convinced of the existence of Stratton. But if this was some act of Kenworthy's to set something up, he was acting it out damned well. There was a moment of embarrassing silence, then he spoke in an almost broken tone.

"I said I'd bring Stratton back. And I did. And believe it or not, I let him get out for a wee-wee, not five miles from here. Did the same myself, with my back to him. Not three seconds, Shiner—how often have I heard a detective-sergeant say that. I don't know how he managed to merge with the landscape. There were two ditches, two folds of dead ground, two lines of hedgerow. I tried the wrong one first, all along the line."

"Is it generally known, sir? Stratton wasn't under arrest, was he?"

"I told you and the Chief Inspector. You didn't believe me, but he did. The Worcestershire police took the trouble to pick him up for us. Your pal Billy Soames brought him to London. Sid Heather kept him happy on the train to Lynn. It's all in the log."

"He'll turn up, sir."

It was a banal thing to say, but the best Wright could manage. And Kenworthy really did lose his temper.

"By God, he'd better, Shiner! By God, he'd better! If, after thirty years, the best I can do is lose the only man who could pull this one out for us—"

"What sort of a man is he, sir?"

"You've read the diary—so you tell me."

"All right, I'll plunge: contemplative, retiring, quiet, diffident—philosophical. Certain rustic chivalry about him. Rather like one side of Charlie's character."

Kenworthy looked at him sharply.

"What's the other side of Charlie's character?"

"I can't get it out of my mind that Charlie might just possibly be quick, crafty, underhand—possibly violent."

"I know one thing, Shiner—Stratton would make a bloody good Indian scout. Shiner—I only looked down to get my glove off, to get at my flies."

"Yes, sir—that time with Albert Boardman—I never could get you to listen—"

"Don't keep on, Shiner, bugger you!"

A minute or two later, without consultation, they crossed the road to the *Red Lion*.

"Is he likely to be dangerous?" Wright asked.

"Gentle as a lamb. That's why I didn't worry when he wanted to pee."

"They why did he cut off?"

"Didn't want to be involved."

"But it seems to me he's very much involved."

"He isn't, Shiner."

"Then I don't get it. I don't get it at all."

"Shiner, I'm ashamed of you."

"Sir—you know something."

"I haven't seen a shred of evidence that you haven't."

"Then, sir. No: I don't get it."

"You ought to be transferred to Traffic, Shiner—not promoted to P Division."

They had reached the forecourt of the pub. Kenworthy made them stand for a moment, and put his hand on Wright's elbow.

"Shiner, not play-acting, straight—who's your candidate?"

"Unless Charlie is indeed a schizophrenic, I'll settle for Joe Margerum."

"That's what I think."

"Joe Margerum with one of the others."

"Correct. Which one?"

"Maurice, Tom or Tennant."

"Could be. And how are we going to get them to tell us?"

"I'm stuck at the moment."

"So am I. But I wasn't at half past eleven this morning. Will Stratton hadn't pleaded his bladder."

"I'm still not with it."

"Then you ought to go back to trying shop-door handles. Let's go and drown the sorrows of P Division."

·17·

"COME TO THE pictures," Kenworthy said. "It might even be up your street—a man of your age and vigor."

Chief Inspector Heather, the single-minded plodder who did much of the London co-ordination when one of the Murder Squad was out in the provinces, had dealt with Cynthia Merridew's flat. A tea-chest of stuff was dispatched to the Report Center, and a rough inventory made of much that was left behind.

There was a folio of obscene eighteenth-century lithographs, the eleven volumes of the monumental (and rare) Victorian labor *My Secret Life*, and Fraxi's *Index Librorum Prohibitorum*. Apart from those, Miss Merridew's library was immense, catholic—and a tribute to her scholarship. Sid Heather had an eye for what was significant. There was a great deal of classical exegesis, and the interpretations of the masters had been copiously and neatly annotated in her own handwriting in the margins. There were several shelves, Heather reported, tightly packed with folk-lore—central European, some of it in exotic languages, likewise annotated by her—as well as East Anglian. There was a comprehensive selection on humdrum teaching method—from the social training of the adolescent to new systems for teaching infants to read; and there was every sign that her interests in the techniques of the profession had continued long after her retirement from the active scene.

This accorded with what a former colleague had to say about her. Heather had brought this man to King's Lynn with him, too, and Kenworthy had a fruity half hour with him. Stooping, cardiganed, approaching his eighties, the old gentleman had also remained encyclopedically and acidly abreast of developments in his previous specialisms. As a time-molded civil servant, he did his best to present a balanced picture with honest care—but also with an exaggerated enjoyment of his own deliberate, minor and slightly cynical indiscretions. With not much time to spare—and with a pleasure in the man's company that expanded from minute to minute—Kenworthy had to pilot him patiently along the course.

The picture of Cynthia Merridew that emerged was four-sided. There was the academic—isolated, incisive, imaginative, way-out, an authority acknowledged by authorities, the center-point of an ever diminishing series of circles, the barely distinguishable but clearly living figure down the wrong end of the telescope.

Then there was the way she had with children—the ability to break through to Pamela Tennant. It was not a science she had learned from psychologists and pedagogues. It was an art innate. From her private heights she could come down to a meticulous concern for trivial detail. She could stop a child from crying on its first morning in a reception class in a rough and tumble primary school on an industrial estate—though the chances were that she would have the headmistress in tears by the mid-morning break.

"And this, you'd maintain," Kenworthy asked, "was the true Cynthia Merridew? Not just a carefully prepared and executed professional pose?"

"Of course it was carefully prepared. A man's whole life is a preparation for tomorrow. And equally carefully executed; she was not the sort of woman who lived from hour to hour by accident. But not a pose, Mr. Kenworthy, that I do assure you."

"A genuine love of children, then?"

It sounded, as he said it, like an infantile over-simplification.

"Love—yes—*concern* was always one of her favorite words—for anyone not capable of looking after themselves."

"Did she ever express concern for a child called Charlie Margerum?"

"I was not of her intimate friends, Superintendent."

"Or a child called Will Stratton?"

"No, Mr. Kenworthy. I would not have expected to have done."

"But how does this accord with her treatment of the headmistress? She had a reputation for blasting into schools like a winnowing wind.''

"Very apposite. She fanned them with fans. Some of us who worked with her sometimes thought she went too far. But it was the complement of the same image. Fools she would suffer, not gladly, but at least with as much patience as she could force upon herself. What she could not tolerate was those who could have helped themselves but wouldn't.''

"She attacked them with a consummate command of cruelty, didn't she? Would you go so far as to call her a sadist?''

"No. Because she didn't enjoy cruelty. The subject fascinated her—as a confessor can be fascinated by sin.''

"I suppose he can. More usually, he comes to take it for granted.''

"Miss Merridew was anything but usual, Mr. Kenworthy. I wish she was here to argue with you. She would tell you that the moment you take evil for granted, you give it a charter to exist.''

"So she took the evil upon herself? Masochism?''

"All these words, Superintendent! At what stage does intellectual curiosity become a vice? She had to understand— she had to identify herself with suffering. If, in the process of investigating, she found a vicarious pleasure—let me put it in a different way. Give her a fragment of poetry, a line unfinished, unbegun even, from the splinter of a Greek vase, and she might, she just might, be able to put in the missing word. Perhaps even more than a word—a phrase, the completion of an image. But into that critical synthesis she was distilling a life-time of power—of linguistic finesse, of archaeological know-how, of poetic inspiration, of identification with an age. When she heard of a man being hanged—''

"She felt she had to undergo the experience.''

"Of course. Because a line of poetry is also an experience— so, come to that, is a Greek vase.''

"Experience meant everything to her?''

"It was important.''

"And sexual experience?''

"If you're asking me whether I slept with her, Mr. Kenworthy, the answer is no.''

He spoke with a wealth of undertones; he did not, he implied, regret the omission.

"What I'm asking rather, is how promiscuous she might have been. Nowadays we say sleep around. Did she?"

"There were limits to our exchanges of confidence. I'll say I think not."

"And on what grounds do you think not?"

"By the same system which completes the line of verse on the shard."

"She wasn't a nympho?"

"Good God, no. She'd never have allowed herself to be anything so untidy."

"Come, come, aren't you playing with terms? Has a nympho any choice?"

"Within those parameters, Superintendent, I can answer you categorically. If a nympho has no choice, then she wasn't one. If a nympho can exercise self-control, then she may possibly have exercised it. She sublimated."

"Into what?"

"Into furious activity—mental, emotional, academic, social, artistic, literary and physical. Also, she liked men. Their company, I mean."

"Would you care to name any?"

"No. I wouldn't care to. It was rumored that there had been a grand love. She was of an age to have lost a man in the trenches. It wouldn't help to name names. They're all dead."

"Thank you," Kenworthy said.

Cynthia Merridew had left nothing in the way of personal notebooks and diaries. There was plenty of manuscript, but it was all concerned with textual criticism or regional legend. There was no wealth of ancient letters—even a scarcity of recent ones; a final warning from the Electricity Board, whose last account she had apparently overlooked, and a monthly statement from a West End store—she had bought herself two new vests and a handbag.

And there was a tape-recording from a machine that stood in mid-stream on a coffee-table, as well as three home-cine films in cartons. Hence the private showing in the darkened caravan trailer.

The first they saw was commercial under-the-counter pornography. Made, to judge by the hair-styles, in the early 1940's, it depicted a couple ejected from a bed by the unexpected arrival of the owner of a flat. Of the scene between the sheets little was shown beyond the man's shoulder-blades, and little of the woman below the salt-cellar. In their rush to escape, the couple had not time to put on anything but their immediate outdoor clothes—a dirty old trench-coat and an improbably opulent fur coat. There was a chase from one shop doorway to another that might have been shot somewhere off the Edgware Road. There were glimpses, less than tantalizing, of a knee under the fur, the tearing open of the coat against the handle of a coster's barrow; an improbable discarding of the garments and a receding shot of unlovely buttocks like an exit by Mickey Mouse.

"I'd like to have seen her face when she saw what she'd bought," Kenworthy said.

"I suppose there's a public for this kind of thing—still."

"Shiner—you know damned well there is. Reps in a hotel bedroom."

The second film was less artificial—and even less artistic. It was an ordinary and unexcogitated sex-act—a barrel-chested young man with sideboards and a jaded whore in black underwear who was obviously bored by the whole proceeding. The cameraman had not contributed much of his potential, and the cutting-room had wasted no overheads on the finer points of continuity.

Wright and Kenworthy were unstirred—exaggerated their indifference in each other's presence. The Norfolk Chief Inspector came into the room in the middle of the showing and undiplomatically treated himself to a hearty chuckle. Even in the darkness, without speaking, an escape of light from the projector catching his profile, Kenworthy managed to convey a stony reception.

"Does it bring you any further forward?" the county man asked, when the lights were up again.

"If everything we touched advanced the case, we'd be back home again by now."

"How often do you think she had a private viewing of that one?"

"Difficult to tell. Perhaps just another disappointing buy. But I wouldn't be certain. It might have given her devious satisfaction."

"At her age?"

"Who knows? Fascinating questions, Chief Inspector. But,

their answers won't butter this slice of bread for us. There isn't time for all we'd like to know. We must resist the temptation."

"Yes, I know—"

The Chief Inspector had an urge to get something off his mind.

"This case has been throwing up a lot of things my way—"

"I know. You can see an end to some local headaches—"

"I don't want to lose the chance, sir. But I'm holding my hand. First things first, I know—"

"You're showing exemplary patience, Chief Inspector. And I'll give you the go-ahead the moment it won't endanger my own little ploy. Is the box-search laid on?"

"Down to the last copper. Concentric cordons moving forward at first light."

"Will Stratton can have a night's rest, then. It's no more than his right, poor devil. Now, Shiner: the other machine. Eight millimeter. I've got a feeling that this is going to be distinctly amateurish."

And it was. Film had obviously been scarce, and the camera had taken some time to settle down in Charlie Margerum's capacious, clumsy, but not entirely insensitive hands. He had set the scene for the mock-up hanging with an ooze of thick, brown water, a curving ripple cutting the edge of a reed-bed, the scaffold beached askew in the mud at the lowest of the ebb. Or perhaps it was Cynthia Merridew herself who had taken the establishing shots. There was a confident steadiness in some that was lacking in others. One panning shot, over to the horizons beyond Hickling's, was beautiful in its own right.

Then the tide was running high, ruffled pools among the sedge, a lap of wavelets against the freeboard of the scaffold. Charlie had tried to take a sequence from a flank, had accidentally tilted the camera so as to black-out the screen for a second with a close-up of the timbering—and then had achieved the angle he wanted, without however considering the grotesque effects of foreshortening. Cynthia Merridew appeared absurdly frail and tiny, between long, converging parallel bars.

Her hands were tied behind her back, her ankles strapped with buckled leather. The noose was loose about her neck, the knot lying on her left shoulder, a loop of slack hanging down to the level of her waist.

Then the drop was shown at falling levels of the tide: the scum and straws thrown up by the retreating water, the swirl of current down a narrow gully, the reducing parabola of the slack rope. And finally the floating bridge was within an inch or two of the mud. Cynthia Merridew was on tiptoe—not straining upwards in an act, but balanced on a ballerina's points, because now she had to be. The camera showed the tautness of the rope against the coping; then Cynthia Merridew's face, composed and concentrated, thin features that could in turn be hypersensitive or mean. Charlie must have leaped forward to release the strain at the last permissible moment. She said something to him, which the camera had registered, thereby dispelling an illusion that had been growing tense. There were two further shots, both trite and ineffective—a swing upwards to settle on a cloud, and then a gull, wheeling over the mud-flats. Then blank film.

"Tells us nothing."

"Except that she was mad."

"A relative term. She was trying to find something out. Perhaps she succeeded. Perhaps she didn't. We could run it through in front of a lip-reader," Kenworthy said. "I like to hear the end of any story. I wonder what that was she said?"

"We could always ask Charlie," Wright suggested. "Are you going to put on a performance for him?"

"It depends on whether we have time to kill tomorrow. If I thought Charlie had done it, I might use this to break him. It would be a unique experience, don't you think?"

"You're sure in your own mind that Margerum's in the clear?"

This was the Chief Inspector. He was only somewhat patchily in Kenworthy's confidence.

"In my own mind, I'm sure who did it. But I've insufficient evidence, and I'm not likely to get any more. I'm so sure of that that I'd almost risk giving up trying. I also need to know who was assistant executioner, and the evidence there is even thinner. But I'm relying on Will Stratton, when we get him back, to cause quite a stir among certain people. Chief Inspector—I want Will Stratton delivered into my hands by eight tomorrow morning at the latest. You do that for me, and you shall have all your Norfolk villains, lock, stock and barrel."

"That's a handsome offer."

"Now this."

There remained the tape recording. She had been in the middle of recording something symphonic. Kenworthy said that it was Beethoven's Fourth. It stopped in the middle of the third movement, and the remainder of the track was virgin. So she had had to switch off for some reason or other—and there was no reason to regard that fact as sinister. The reverse was mostly taken up by a talk on B.B.C.3 about new archaeological theories based on a dig in Crete. There was also, towards the end, a jig-saw of similar bits and pieces: a scene from *Cymbeline*, a tag of Smetana quartet, a speaker from the Open University on Florentine sculpture. This was interrupted by the telephone, and Cynthia Merridew's voice, distant and elderly, informing someone that he had a wrong number.

"Nothing," Kenworthy said. "Let's go to bed."

·18·

ALL THE NATIONAL dailies the next morning contained an Identikit synthesis of Will Stratton. *If you see this man—*

Height five feet nine; aged seventy-four, but could pass himself off as sixty; weight eleven and a half stone; dark eyes, swarthy complexion; gypsy-like features; probably unshaven, and likely to bear the marks of sleeping rough.

Even in the flatness of the portrait, there was a remarkable resemblance to Charlie Margerum. And it was obvious to Wright that in making up the picture, Kenworthy had relied very heavily on the uniformed photograph from the First World War. It was, in fact, clearly the same man—and nothing surprising in that.

But there was something, somewhere, that did not fit. Wright could not put his finger on it; it was something thrown up by his detective's instinct for significant inconsistencies. Kenworthy was up to something. The newspaper accounts of Will Stratton contained no reference to the fact that he had escaped from escort. And Wright was not surprised at this. Kenworthy would not be anxious to publicize his handling of the incident— and as Will Stratton was not under arrest, nor likely to be, he could hardly be posted as a danger to the community. But Kenworthy had not told all, even to Wright. There was something incredibly inefficient in the way he had carried on yesterday—and he had not mentioned it again after his outburst on the way back from Charlie's boat. He had not, after that, even seemed particularly disturbed about it—and Wright knew well enough what it was like when Kenworthy was disturbed. Even this morning he was not on tenterhooks—as he should have been, according to form. It was already two minutes after the eight o'clock deadline he had given the Chief Inspector, and he had not even looked at his watch.

So Wright was beginning to wonder whether Will Stratton existed at all—except as a counter in Kenworthy's game.

And Kenworthy nodded at the newspaper propped against the tea-pot.

"I'd give anything to see Joe Margerum's face when he picks that up from the mat this morning."

It seemed to confirm Wright's suspicions.

"He's not, of course, sir, the only one left in Mawson's Drove with first-hand memory of Will Stratton."

"Indeed, no. But we can't be on hand to see all their reactions. I expect we shall get to hear of anything that matters."

He sounded relaxed and unconcerned.

Breakfast with Kenworthy loomed large in Wright's recollections of case-work: especially breakfast on the last morning, when there was often a lull, and the knowledge that the case was going to break. Wright could not ever remember Kenworthy allowing himself to be rushed over the first meal of the day. More than once he had heard him attribute his general run of rude health to his respect for his digestion: which was perfect nonsense, because at any other time of day—or night— he could show an absolute disregard for what he ate—or how and when.

Wright associated with the smell of marmalade on toast the chief's disquisitions—sometimes whimsical, often exploratory, never conventional—on the current state of play. But this morning was different. The setting was familiar enough: a quiet corner in the dining-room of a pub. An intangible expectancy was in the air; an assurance that today would be the day. Kenworthy's mood was characteristic: restful, sardonic, refusing to be rushed. But he did not want to go on discussing the case. He suddenly switched to the internal politics of P Division.

"I don't know who it is you'll be replacing. It must be either Riley or Clayton who's going. You'll need a good head for depths, Shiner."

"Gradually acquiring one."

Kenworthy turned to the back page.

"Blast! I fancied *Pamplemousse* at Wincanton. Just didn't get a chance to get on the blower."

"Sir."

"Yes?"

He appeared not to wish to be drawn away from the day's runners.

"Sir—there's something you haven't told me."

"Quite a lot, Shiner."

"Well, sir—"

"I do have a private life, you know. I didn't tell you what we had for dinner last Sunday. I didn't tell you what my wife said—"

"Sir!"

"You're under the impression, then, that—"

"About the case, I mean."

"Oh, the case. Yes, about the case. What do you think I haven't told you about the case, then?"

"About Will Stratton."

"Do you have to keep reminding me?"

But there was no fire behind the mock anger. He was playing his exasperating game.

"Is there a Will Stratton?" Wright asked. "Or have you invented all this, including a box-search that's going to find no one, just to get that picture into twelve million newspapers, including the one that's going to be delivered this morning at Candle Mere Farm?"

"When the question of your promotion came up, I told them you had imagination, Shiner."

"And that's all you're going to tell me? Sir—years ago, when I was a sergeant—"

"You still are a sergeant, Shiner—till you get to P Division."

"Yes, sir."

Double silence. Then Kenworthy returned.

"You'll give me better service, Shiner, if we leave things as they are for the present. Have you ever been on the inside of an internal inquiry, within the force, Shiner—at the wrong end of the questions, I mean?"

"No, sir."

"I'm going to be, if this goes wrong. But I've stocked you up with an impenetrable defense. You didn't know. See?"

Then the Chief Inspector came into the room. It was the first time he had dared approach Kenworthy at the meal-table. Kenworthy called for an extra cup and saucer.

"Got him?"

"Not yet, sir."

Now Kenworthy did look at his watch.

"Quarter past, Chief Inspector."

"We're working as fast as we can. Some of these farm groups can't just be walked over. Three sections have finished. Four are nearly through."

"And not a sign?"

"Not as much as a hollow in the grasses."

"You haven't moved out towards the marshes yet?"

"No, sir."

The Chief Inspector seemed surprised at the question.

"We agreed—"

"Of course."

"We've blocks on every road, north, west, and south. Somebody or other has his field-glasses on every yard of the perimeter. If we have flushed him out, we shall push him towards the sea. It'll take longer than we thought."

"Then it'll take longer than I thought to turn those poachers over to you."

"I understand that. In any case, I shan't have time."

"But you don't want to lose time, either, do you, Chief Inspector? Those poachers—"

"Sir?"

"You'll find, I think, that something a bit juicier than poaching's been going on—"

"That, sir, is what—"

"Shall I tell you one or two other little ideas that I've had, Chief Inspector?"

The county officer suddenly understood that he was about to hear something out of the ordinary, and began to look suitably interested. Kenworthy asked the waitress for another pot.

"Poaching there has been. Large scale. All sorts of technical gadgetry. Conducted like a military campaign."

"So much we've known for months."

"Oddly enough, I think you were meant to. This was military precision, and I fancy you're going to find a military mind behind it. Hence, the new bungalow, the facade of women's romances—which are probably fairly lucrative in themselves.

But not so rewarding as drugs, illegal immigrants, arms for terrorists, traffic in agitators, or whatever is sheltering behind a lesser crime. I've no doubt you'll find those poacher-witnesses are Tennant's satellites. That's how he was able to control their evidence. You see, I think they really did serve him up something out of the blue. I believe they genuinely did see movement down the Leam that night. They saw the van, the scaffold in the mist, the bundle that was the corpse. They saw a man they thought was Charlie. It might even have been Charlie—we're not clean certain of this one yet. They told Tennant, and the chance was too good to him. It was so good that he didn't take the time to think it out carefully.''

"They all trip up sooner or later."

Kenworthy did not like the interruption, and pretended it had not happened.

"Because Tennant wants to be rid of Charlie—for all sorts of reasons, personal, family and just plain villainous. My guess is that when you start stretching the rack on Tennant, he'll try to make a lot of his partnership with Charlie. But I wouldn't be too impressed, if I were you—unless you unearth new evidence. I think that Charlie has been very helpful to some of Tennant's little schemes. Because, in a general sort of way, he's a very helpful sort of bloke, is Charlie. He's reasonably careful about the law—but he doesn't accept it spontaneously, if you see what I mean. But that's not been nearly as helpful as the bit of land he owns. Tennant's bungalow is well placed—for a man who wants alibis, and a short approach to the main theater. But it's Marsh Hall Farm that counts. Charlie's the best sited eccentric for many a mile of coast.''

"The Leam, the standing-stages, the dead ground—"

"I think you'll find that the new boat belongs to Tennant. Charlie merely garages it for him. He didn't tell us so, because we were careful not to ask. I think he'll prevaricate when we do, or at least, when you do—because I shan't. I value my friendship with Charlie, and I don't want to spoil it. Incidentally, I can't prove any of this. You might find a bill of sale for the boat somewhere. You'll probably find it easier to look into who paid for the new lock. And all this, Chief Inspector, is pure conjecture. I can afford to do a bit of guessing, because this isn't my case. All this secret of the swamp stuff is yours. This is your patch, and you're bloody well welcome to it.''

"Thank you, sir."

"And you make no move, Chief Inspector, till I drive to the city with two friends, one of whom I forecast will be Joe Margerum. Otherwise you'll start cross-currents that might disturb my own rather delicate machinations. And now—what time is your front line fanning out?"

The Chief Inspector looked a little ashamed of himself.

"Ten o'clock, sir."

"Good. That gives me a bit of time to catch up with the admin."

But Kenworthy, seldom eager to wage war with a wire basket, was to be denied access to the paperwork for yet another hour or so. As the three policemen walked into the headquarter's compound, acknowledging the salute of the uniformed constable stamping his feet at the gate, they observed all the signs of anticipation that are shown by men accustomed to discipline their excitement. Each pair of eyes was raised momentarily from the job it was doing to look at Kenworthy, to savor his reaction. Wright was familiar with the syndrome. Something had come up within the last few minutes. For a space of minutes, the most junior rank present knew something that the man at the top had still to learn. Wright sensed it, and wanted to push all the supernumeraries out of the way, to get into a corner, just the three of them, with whatever new incident had come to light. The Chief Inspector sensed it, and scanned the compound uneasily, trying to spot in advance the weak link in his organization that could frustrate an improvised operation. Kenworthy sensed it, and elaborately ignored it, marching toward his office trailer as if only his desk could save the whole investigation from chaotic collapse.

The center of the tension was a patrol-car that had driven in just ahead of them, its rear wheels side-stepping in the mud. An officer held the door open for the passenger, a small man with features rather like a pike, and bulbous eyes behind strong lenses.

"Dr. Wilshaw, sir."

Kenworthy chose to appear no more than casually interested.

"Sir—he's not very pleased. He's had to put off a lecture he was going to give in Sheffield this afternoon."

Kenworthy looked at the man as if his presence was faintly distasteful.

"I'll see him in five minutes."

Dr. Wilshaw stepped forward, his lower lip sagging, his nostrils stiffened aggressively.

"You'll see me now. Or I shall leave at once. I understand that I am here voluntarily—"

"All right—I'll see you now."

Kenworthy spoke as if he did not care one way or the other. The four men crowded into his personal office space.

"If you'd come forward at the proper time, you'd have been able to go to Sheffield or anywhere else you like."

"I have been away from home. When I returned last night and looked at my accumulated newspapers, I went at once to my local police-station and made a deposition. It was painstaking and exhaustive. I have nothing to add to it. It is explicit on all points that can interest you."

Kenworthy looked at the Chief Inspector.

"Has it arrived?"

"I'll go and see."

"One of Miss Merridew's main reasons for traveling out to East Anglia was to keep an appointment with you, Dr. Wilshaw?"

"One only of her reasons."

"I don't think we need quibble on that point. But tell us why she wanted to see you. Or was it you who wanted to see her?"

"I am a scholar, Superintendent. So was she."

"You met regularly?"

"No. Rarely. And, perhaps I might add, impersonally. Not a dozen times in our careers, and then usually over the floor of a conference hall. Sometimes we needed to consult each other's specialisms."

"And what is yours?"

"Pre-Conquest folk-right."

"We understand that she was interested in some new discovery in the Fosdyke area—"

The Chief Inspector came in with a buff folder.

"Brought in by motorcyclist during the night."

It contained a page and a half typed statement. Kenworthy appeared to digest it in a glance. Wilshaw waited until he had finished.

"You will find all the relevant facts there."

"It says nothing here about Fosdyke."

"Fosdyke is not relevant."

"Allow me to judge that. What has been found at Fosdyke? An early threshing engine, I believe?"

"That is not what interested her. There are also the foundations, possibly the filled-in crypt, of a Saxon chapel. Cannibalized by generations of peasants and concealed beyond recognition under a fifteenth-century barn."

It irritated Dr. Wilshaw to be made to talk. His nose and receding jaw looked more than ever like the snout of a predatory fish.

"And Miss Merridew was anxious to know about this? To use it?"

"Of course."

"Why 'of course'?"

"Because she was a scholar, and East Anglia was one of her spheres."

Kenworthy looked at him as if he were weighing up something several steps removed from the immediate topic.

"There are grades and varieties of scholar, Dr. Wilshaw. I would imagine that Miss Merridew's approach to medieval history was different, for example, from yours."

"Of course. There is more than one type of brush-work on any canvas."

"Miss Merridew's interpretation was essentially subjective?"

"That is true."

And it was equally true, Wright thought, that Wilshaw's life work must be desiccated and ferociously accurate, definitive and shorn of magic or enthusiasm.

"So let's cut out all the middle game," Kenworthy said. "Just tell me what was her personal approach to the new find at Fosdyke."

Wilshaw cleared his throat.

"Miss Merridew was a romantic. Her identification with the past was inspirational. It is an unreliable method—but I would be the last to deny our indebtedness to some of its more felicitous strokes."

"There's no need to make excuses for her. Just tell us what you didn't bother to put in the deposition."

Wilshaw coughed nervously.

"Supererogatory. Obviously you know already. She was interested in trial by ordeal."

"Trial by ordeal?"

"Fire and water. In this case, primarily fire. Holding hot iron. As perhaps you know, until it was forbidden by the Lateran Council in the thirteenth century, this savage device of primitive justice was reserved to the administration of the priesthood. In fact, until the Conquest relegated it to a pit or trench outside, the trial took place within the church itself. Miss Merridew had conceived the notion, amalgamating legends, that St. Athelstan's at Fosdyke had been prolifically the scene of such tortures. I am by no means certain that she was right. But I take it that the actual details of historical controversy would be superfluous to your inquiry—?"

Kenworthy permitted himself to smile.

"We'd be more interested to know what she wanted to do about it."

"Oh!"

Wilshaw was impatient, embarrassed and disgusted at the memory.

"She wanted to stage a characteristic trial *in situ.*"

"With your help?"

"It would have to come to that, if I had allowed myself to become embroiled. In the first instance, my involvement was limited to helping her to gain access. The supposed chapel is on private property. I promised that I would arrange for her to view it."

"But this other thing?"

Wilshaw spread his hands.

"I do not know whether she would have pursued it to its culmination or not. She certainly brimmed over with enthusiasm. Charisma. She was like that. Though I have never seen her quite so moved."

Wilshaw paused. He did not feel adequate to describing the situation.

"You think she was mad?" Kenworthy asked.

"I think that she was totally committed to anything into which she inquired. In this case, she wanted to propose herself as the subject of a trial by fire. She was to be accused of something of which she knew herself to be innocent. And I think, Superintendent—she was not explicit about the details and far be it from me to have pressed her—I had the impression that it stemmed from some accusation that had been made against her in the past.''

''You mean that she wanted to use this as an exercise in psychoanalysis?''

''No. She wanted a valid setting for a trial by ordeal. Whatever it was, it was something that rankled. I was sensitive to that. But that was not the whole point. For such a trial there had to be an indictment. It had to be real. And for her to withstand the torture, she had to be innocent of it.''

He took out a snuff-box, offered to the others, who declined, and took a pinch from the back of his hand.

''The priest—it had to be a priest, and it was some comfort to me that I did not think she would find one who would co-operate—would take from a brazier with tongs a small red hot cylinder of iron, which he would deposit in her palm. She would hold it thus while he slowly counted to three, when he would remove it. He would then bandage her hand and arm, seal the dressing, and let it remain thus for three days and nights. If, when the bandage was removed, there was no more harm done than a blister no larger than half a walnut, then she was to be adjudged guiltless.''

''And you think she had the guts to go through with that?''

''Undoubtedly—though at her age—''

''Simply to recreate historical authenticity?''

''More importantly, to test her own *mana*.''

''*Mana*?''

''The strong heart. The anthropologists have adopted a Maori term. Perhaps that is not without some significance. A mysterious power, bestowed by confidence. I think she honestly believed that she would not blister at all.''

The Chief Inspector looked at his watch.

''Sir—if you'll excuse me—''

''Before you go—fix me up with a personal radio—''

''Certainly.''

But the Chief Inspector was anything but pleased at the delay. He had left his departure for the next stage of the search to the last possible moment.

''You won't mind if I leave young Jevons to fix it for you?''

''Of course not—''

And Kenworthy returned his attention to Wilshaw.

"So. You came over to Mawson's Drove to meet her."

"Because she telephoned me. Her car was off the road for an hour or two. I drove us to a restaurant near Holbeach, where we talked over lunch. And then I brought her back here, where, at her request, I set her down on a road between two farms. I would gladly have taken her to her destination—but she was most emphatic that she wanted to pay her calls on foot, for nostalgic reasons. That was the last I saw of her."

"At least, you managed to stave off any final commitment on the Fosdyke affair."

Dr. Wilshaw permitted himself the first suspicion of a smile they had seen.

"If she had not met with this appalling business, she would not have been so easy to fob off. She promised me—and I fear that I looked upon it rather as a threat—that she would be returning in the spring. She had unearthed some character, a man called Stratton—I remember the name because, quite absurdly, she seemed to think I would know it. I could never get her to remember that this is not my home neighborhood."

"Stratton—"

"That's right. She seemed to think that his arrival here would cause something of a stir."

"I'm banking on that, too."

That was all, except for formalities. Kenworthy called a desk-sergeant.

"There's a gentleman here who has to be in Sheffield directly after lunch. Make sure we do everything we can."

Then he reached for his overcoat.

"Come on, Shiner. I think we may be in on something interesting."

They walked out of the village along a road that was becoming as familiar as a second home to them: a brewer's lorry was delivering at the *Red Lion*; from the windows of the school they heard the children singing *Greensleeves*; a young married woman with a scarf around her head was cycling towards the outskirts with a shopping basket lashed behind her saddle.

A car-load of policemen overtook them. This must be the last of the Chief Inspector's redeployed army. When they reached the edge of the marsh, they could see on either hand the arc of uniformed men, drawn up and ready to move out toward the sea.

"At least, they won't have far to look. He's not troubling to conceal his presence. Poor devil's probably cold."

Kenworthy pointed. Over in the middle distance, between the hidden course of the Leam and the equally uncertain line of the coast, the ramshackle hutment that was known as Hickling's stood our gray amid the mingled browns and greens. From its chimney a thin line of slate-blue smoke rose at an angle, hung inert at a certain layer of the upper air, then dissipated imperceptibly from its upper edges.

"It might be him," Wright conceded.

"Who else?"

"Fowlers?"

Kenworthy shook his head. He switched on his portable transmitter.

"Hullo, control. K. here. Seen that? No smoke without fire. Code-word Casemate, then—"

So Kenworthy had not left it all to the Chief Inspector. He was familiar with the detailed plan of the search, its phasing and its codes. What time had he got up this morning?

"Come, Shiner, I'd like to be fairly close to this—but not close enough to get in anybody's way."

They set off across the difficult ground, waiting until the cordon had first moved off, and remaining a few yards behind the line of advance, a delay not difficult to achieve, since the terrain was so treacherous that only thigh-boots would have allowed movements straight ahead. When they reached the bank of the Leam, swollen by the rising tide, Wright took a run and jumped the channel landing in water deeper and colder than he had expected. Kenworthy walked in search of a narrower crossing.

"Feeling independent, Shiner?"

"Sir?"

"Hullo, control. Kenworthy here. There's no point in all this line abreast stuff. Everybody will get wet feet, and two are enough. Hold everybody where they are. Send one man and one dog in from the left, and I'll send my sergeant in from here. Tell the dog-handler to take his time from Wright—so that they both go in together."

Wright was suddenly glad of the freedom and activity. For thirty yards he followed a patch of rough but solid turf where it was possible to walk in normal fashion. He saw the dog-handler negotiating a gully, a black Doberman Pinscher bitch at his heel, the leash across the back of his knee in training-ground fashion. There were about another eighty yards to go.

And then something struck the water, a few yards to his left. Simultaneously there was a puff of smoke from the window of the hut, the report of a sporting-gun. Wright flung himself forward on to his belly. At the same time, he saw the dog-handler stoop to release the animal. Then there was another shot, this time at the dog, missing by a generous margin.

Kenworthy shouted, abandoning the radio net.

"Come back—both of you! Call the dog in! Call her in! I'm not risking man or animal for Will Stratton. We've got time—he hasn't."

Wright rolled over, turned around and began propelling himself back to their base-line on his elbows. The small of his back felt hollow. He dared not raise his head to look over his shoulder. He could not be certain that his silhouette was below the visibility line. But there were no more shots. A clamor of herring-gulls, outraged by the gun and the unfamiliar mass visitation, screamed and whined overhead.

Wright crawled to where Kenworthy and the Chief Inspector had come together in a convenient and safe depression. To right and left the men of the cordon all had their heads down. There was no sign of movement anywhere. Reaction had been quick and efficient.

"No need to panic," Kenworthy was saying. "No need for anything but patience. I don't think he'll stir before nightfall. By then we'll have moved enough men in to close cover to stop all his earths. If it comes to the crunch, we'll starve him out. I'm certainly not taking any risks. I'll not risk scratching a man's arm for this character."

"Issue arms to half a dozen marksmen, just in case?"

"Not yet, Chief Inspector—not for a long time yet. I don't think it will come to that—and Shiner: better get back and put something dry on. I don't want to hand you over to P Division with a running nose."

"Bit of a surprise, sir—"

"Nothing," Kenworthy answered solemnly, "is ever a surprise."

·19·

IT WOULD BE an exaggeration to say that one could smell the moth-balls in Charlie Margerum's best suit—but the thought sprang to mind. It was a dark charcoal gray in a cloth too heavy to hold the trouser-creases properly and he was wearing a coarse white shirt with vertical blue stripes that must have been pre-war.

The day had sagged in the middle after the questioning of Dr. Wilshaw. There was documentation in the wake of an inter-force inquiry that was unimagined by readers of newspaper reports: time-sheets for attached personnel, expense accounts, vehicle work-sheets. And though much of this was churned out at clerical level, Kenworthy always liked his sergeant to keep a running eye on the pattern. The aftermath could be formidable, and though any attempt at premature completion was bound to be frustrated, it paid to try to keep abreast. Glory could be tarnished, long after a case was closed, by the bloody-mindedness of an internal auditor.

So Wright spent the inside of the day pecking at a desk-load of paper. In the lunch-hour he strolled out toward the marsh road—but the scene was now remarkable only for its utter inactivity. Somewhere among the sedges a work-force of at least a hundred officers had gone to ground, their immobility so efficient that no casual motorist would have suspected their presence. Even the smoke from Hickling's stove-pipe had vanished. But no man could move from the hut without being observed by a hundred pairs of eyes, and provided that the ring was eventually tightened with a reasonable touch of imagination at the right stage of twilight, there was little danger that Stratton would escape the net.

But Wright reflected that if he had the ultimate responsibility for the case—as he would, before long, be conducting cases in his own right in P Division—he would have at least one rifle, in a steady pair of hands, trained across the reeds when the final wave went in. But there was no arguing with Kenworthy—and, in any case, the whole thing now bore the appearance of a massive Kenworthy ploy, as if he was just waiting for the monstrous laughter to which he would treat them all when the chestnuts were out in the hearth.

But he wasn't laughing yet. Self-satisfied, that was the word for his present mood. Kenworthy spent a lot of the afternoon chatting inconsequentially with the wireless operator in whose office Wright had read Maud Franklin's diary. He did not talk much to Wright—and Wright was uncomfortably aware that he was not admitted to a private discussion that went on for three-quarters of an hour between the Superintendent and the Chief Inspector. In all the cases that they had worked together, it was the first time that Wright could remember playing second fiddle to a county man. And he did not like it. It felt disconcertingly like not being trusted.

Kenworthy explained it afterwards, when the time came for brief assessment and minimal apologies.

"I kept you in the dark, as I told you I had to, because that was your alibi. I had to tell the other chap—because I had to give him a chance to pull out if he didn't like it."

Late in the afternoon, Kenworthy drove out of the compound, and did not invite Wright to accompany him. He was away about an hour, and when he returned there was some of the characteristic briskness about him that had been lacking since their return from the marsh this morning. He button-holed a Norfolk plain-clothes sergeant.

"Go up to Candle Mere Farm—sensitively—and you'll find one of your colleagues keeping a general eye on things from an unobtrusive corner of the yard. Go and give him a hand—mainly to see that Margerum senior doesn't miss a date I've made with him. If he's not with the family party when they drive down to Charlie's place, between seven and eight, bring him down there yourself. If he tries to side-slip you, arrest him. But I don't think he'll give you any trouble. He hasn't much safety margin, but I think he'll play along with me for a while yet."

And Kenworthy was right. Joe Margerum came. Maurice

and Mavis came. Tom and Sally came. The Tennants came—late, and grumbling about the difficulty they had had in finding a babysitter for Pamela.

They had all dressed for the occasion—none of them as disastrously as Charlie. Mavis, raw-faced and bucolic, was wearing pearls, Maurice a lounge-suit that had not been out many times since it was new. Tom was in a slim fitting suit of Italian cut. Tennant's was tailor-made. Sally had risked an Edwardian smock and a long skirt with a dark floral pattern.

Kenworthy and Wright arrived half an hour before any of the other guests. The Chief Inspector came with them, some other officer, apparently accredited with military experience, having been left in charge of operations on the marsh.

"A long time since you entertained the family on this scale," Kenworthy said.

And Charlie immediately reached for the appropriate volume of his diary.

"I wouldn't go reading any of your poetic code-names to us now. The Chief Inspector here is likely to be taking a professional interest in that side of things from now on. He's going to ask quite a lot of questions that you won't like answering. I can't stop him—and I wouldn't want to if I could."

Charlie nodded, almost vacantly. He had shaved close and his complexion was ashen.

"If I were you, I wouldn't lean too far out of the vertical to shelter that brother-in-law of yours. I don't know what you two have been up to—but he won't do much for you, when we get him in the hot seat—"

"I won't, Mr. Kenworthy."

"Is that a promise, Charlie?"

"That's a promise."

The Tom Margerums were the first to arrive. Sally played up to the occasion as if without effort, taking a credible interest in a print of hare-coursers that Charlie had on his wall.

"I've never seen this before. Has it always been here?"

"He's got so much bloody junk in here," Tom said, "he keeps finding things himself that he didn't know he'd got."

Then he turned to Kenworthy.

"How long is this going to take?"

"Until I can leave with what I want."

"Tom's in the clear," Sally said quietly.

"You've been carrying out an inquiry of your own, have you, Mrs. Margerum?"

"I'll say she has," Tom said.

"I'll make no bones about it, Margerum. It's your Monday midnight conference with your father that I don't like."

"And I didn't like it, either."

"I may well be asking you for a statement."

"I hope you won't."

"I wish I could say, I hope I don't either," Kenworthy said. "But why the hell should I worry about your family loyalties?"

"Why should you indeed?"

It was either ham-acting or sincerity; perhaps a combination of the two. Sally spoke up.

"You'll get what you want in the next half hour, Superintendent, without having to turn the heat on Tom."

And since Tom did not trouble to deny the implications of this, Wright wondered why Kenworthy didn't tighten up his case at once. Perhaps he was looking forward a little too keenly to the play-out of his own script.

"Just one question, then, at this stage," he said gently. "When your father called you over to Candle Mere that night—was it just you? Or a family council?"

"Just me."

"Maurice wasn't present?"

"He'd gone to bed."

"And you said no?"

"What do you bloody think?"

Then Maurice and his wife and the old man arrived. Charlie busied himself deploying a battery of home-made wines and an arsenal of glasses that ranged from eighteenth-century twisted stems to petrol-pump give-aways.

Maurice hardly spoke to his half-brother; Joe Margerum demonstratively ignored him; Mavis was silent and detached from everything and everyone—perhaps studiously so, or perhaps it was intolerable embarrassment. Not one of the three would accept a drink from Charlie.

"So," Kenworthy said, "Maurice had gone to bed?"

And Maurice looked up, startled at the mention of his name. He had no idea what they had been talking about. Tom frowned and looked past Kenworthy.

"So. If Maurice had gone to bed, and Tom was sent for,

rified. The door opened and a man came round it, but did not advance further into their midst. He was swarthy, gypsy-like, dark avised, looked as if he had slept rough the previous night. The resemblance to Charlie Margerum was remarkable; to the First-War portrait of Will Stratton it was even more so. And whoever had done the Identikit likeness had cheated—he had had the original in front of him. There was only one thing inconsistent; but most of the people here had no logical eye for fact at this very moment. Mavis Margerum swung around in her chair and shrieked at her father-in-law.

"You damned old swine. You told me—"

Wright could picture it now: Cynthia Merridew, too frail to take on the pair of them. The old man was no weakling, and Mavis Margerum had done tough jobs about farms all her life.

"Thank you, madam," Kenworthy said. "He could only get help from an in-law, could he? What was it you didn't want: the family scandal? Plus the chance of putting Charlie away for a very long time? Plus a father-in-law who'd have to see things your way for the rest of his life? Oh, and Margerum—"

He went close to the old man, who looked up at him without shifting his position in his chair.

"You owe this young man the sum of £234. That's eighteen years at five shillings a week—the amount his father wasn't able to pay into the Post Office for him. But nobody's going to charge you with Will Stratton's murder. We don't know where you buried him, though I'll bet it's a long way from where his spectacles and razor were found. Not to worry. Cynthia Merridew will do for the time being. Come on, Shiner: you and I can manage these two."

"I'll give you a hand," the Chief Inspector said.

"I rather think you've got some unfinished business on the county file. Sorry, Charlie. Don't let the Major saddle you with too much of the blame."

take a fair time for a man who doesn't know the way. Hullo, Control. Hullo, Control. Here Kenworthy. You can stand down all sections except those on either side of Stratton. They can continue to press him this way."

There followed a silence rather like that of a Quaker Meeting after the settling down of the shuffling bottoms and the creaking shoes. A long, intricate and uncontrolled gurgle came from somebody's digestive system. Wright thought that it was Mavis.

After three minutes, that must have seemed like an hour to some, Sally spoke.

"I don't think I quite understand this, Superintendent."

"I wouldn't expect you to. You're not one of them."

"Well—can't we discuss this? We might be stuck here till midnight at least. And I for one—"

"Sally—"

Kenworthy addressed her as he might have done a member of his own family. They heard Kate breathe in and out.

"Sally—don't try to spoil this for me. I'm enjoying this."

There was a long pause before she answered.

"I'm not."

"But there's someone in this circle who's enjoying it even less than you are. See what I mean? Let's give Will Stratton a chance, shall we?"

And so it went till twenty-three minutes to eleven, which hour Wright recorded precisely in his note-book. Charlie pricked up his ears. Almost everyone in the room came to the alert; here a shoulder, there an arm, an ankle or a wrist was flexed. A distant door opened. Wright made to rise.

"Sit still, Sergeant. He'll find his own way in."

The Chief Inspector changed the crossing of his legs. Footsteps came along the corridor. A door was tried and closed again, and then another. The steps approached the room in which they were sitting.

"Oh, God!" Kate said.

"Superintendent—stop this play-acting!" Tennant urged.

"Be quiet, you!"

The door handle turned, Tom, who was sitting where he could not easily see it, had to slew round to look over his shoulder. Charlie Margerum, the only one who had been moving about in the room throughout the evening, now stood pet-

by, sections eight and nine—he's going to try to slip between you. If he gets to the bank, we could lose him.''

Wright recognized the voice of the wireless operator—Kenworthy's pal. The deception was transparent—to Wright; with the others it was a hundred per cent effective. So there wasn't a Will Stratton: only an intricate stage-management.

And something else came to Wright. Kenworthy hadn't kept him in the dark just to preserve him from trouble if the ploy went wrong. With Wright fooled they were all fooled. Kenworthy had even had him shot at this morning—by a police marksman, or by a marksman seconded to the police, who had been briefed to fire at least five degrees off him and the dog, once they were far enough ahead of the cordon to protect them from strays. The bastard! Wright looked at Kenworthy, and as if reading his mind, Kenworthy looked back at him and smiled his silkiest.

''Hullo, Control. Kenworthy here. Don't panic, Control. Don't do anything, in fact, except let him think he's still being hounded. Don't hinder him from crossing the Leam. We've quite an adequate reception committee waiting for him here.''

He put down the set.

''Haven't we, ladies and gentlemen? And we know that he'll come here, don't we? We know that Will Stratton will come here. Why are we so sure he'll do that, ladies and gentlemen? Would you like me to tell you?''

Sally Margerum, as if suddenly conscious of her relaxed pose, straightened her body in her chair.

''Because he had only one friend in Mawson's Drove, ladies and gentlemen—his son. But why should he have left it until now, I wonder, to come back and square things up, over forty years later, with the man who had murdered him—or thought he had?''

Mavis's eyes moved. She was trying to see her father-in-law's face, but not being able to do so without turning her head, she abandoned the attempt.

''Shall I tell you, ladies and gentlemen?''

Tom looked Kenworthy in the eye. Kate moved as if to speak to Tennant, then thought better of it.

''Because of Cynthia Merridew,'' Kenworthy said. ''Work that one out! Build us up a good fire, Charlie. We shall likely be here a while yet. From Mawson's Leam, in the dark, will

"About your guilt, Joseph Margerum"—he might have been embarking on an after-dinner speech among his professional peers—"I have been in little doubt since I first met you, and in no doubt at all since one particular member of your family talked to my sergeant. You murdered Cynthia Merridew because of something she knew—or, at least, that you thought she knew. What I do not yet know is which of these people here present helped you to incarcerate her in some attic, cellar or disused pig-sty for most of Monday night and the whole of Tuesday—and then to strap her ankles, thong her wrists, slip the knot under her ear and pushed her through the trap in Charlie's granary. I have already remarked that the late lamented public executioner was not expected to do it all himself."

He looked around expectantly, then changed his expression to that of a man who could bear his disappointment philosophically. Old Margerum was breathing through his mouth in rather noisy jerks, Maurice was holding his features rigid. Mavis was staring in front of her, flushed spots about her cheekbones showing through the cosmetics. Tom Margerum turned his eyes, but not his head, to try to see Charlie. Charlie stretched out his hand for the dead-nettle bottle, topped up his glass, and then with a gesture offered it to the others. There were no takers. Sally was studying the contour of her knees. Tennant drummed with his finger-tips on the arm of his chair, realized he was doing it, and stopped. His wife closed her eyes, held them shut for seconds, then opened them again.

"Hullo, Control. Kenworthy. Situation, please."

He turned up the volume—and the answer was not only louder, but clearer than anything they had heard on the set so far.

"Could you ask again in five minutes' time, sir, please—we're just going in."

Sally took a deep breath and exhaled slowly. Charlie turned away from them and attended to the fire. Mavis raised a hand, fingered her pearls, then dropped her fingers back into her lap. It was as if each of them—Charlie excepted—regarded the slightest movement as self-incriminatory.

There was the click of a switch on the radio. A new voice came in, very loud indeed, and crystal clear in its enunciation.

"Get after him, you fool. You've let him get through. Stand

that after he had unsuccessfully asked Maurice and Tom to serve as assistant hangman, he then came to you."

"Who did?"

"Your father-in-law."

Wright looked at Joe Margerum, who was sitting with his hands on his knees, his eyes focused on nothing in particular, his face as expressionless as he could make it. Yet even in that moment, he managed to preserve a conscious dignity. He was still the man who had ridden up in immaculate cavalry boots.

"That's pitching it a bit thick, isn't it, Superintendent? Isn't that tantamount to an accusation—in front of all these witnesses?"

"Ah, yes," Kenworthy said sweetly. "Let's do things in their proper order."

He raised his bottom from the chair, stretched over and slapped Joe Margerum in almost friendly fashion on his thigh.

"Joseph Margerum, I am arresting you for the murder of Cynthia Anne Merridew between the hours of midnight and dawn on—"

He went through the essentials of the cautionary formula politely, and with a lack of pomp that verged on gaiety.

"Does that satisfy all the sticklers? And may I now repeat my original question to you, Major Tennant? I suppose it was after his own family had declined to help him that he came to you?"

"I simply refuse to participate in this absurd dialogue in front of all these people. If you have essential questions to ask, and will have the courtesy to ask me in private—"

"Were you the executioner's assistant?"

"Of course not."

"Was it suggested to you that you should be?"

"Of course not."

"Then I do not know what you are making all this fuss about. You have now fully assured me."

Kenworthy looked with serene satisfaction at the faces of them each in turn. He seemed determined not to relapse into gravity. Presumably he wanted to provoke someone to the point of outburst. Presumably, Wright had also from an early date leaned to the theory that when Kenworthy was walking the boards, the only audience that really interested him was himself.

that means Maurice must already have said no. That leaves . . .
No. Let's leave it till the others come. Let's see what's on the
other channel—''

From somewhere on the floor beside the chair, Kenworthy
produced his radio, switched it on and drew out the aerial.
There was a good deal of static and an exchange of inaudible
voices. Kenworthy put the thing up to his ear.

A scrambled and metallic answer came through. It could not
have been intelligible to anyone in the room. Wright wondered
what sort of an idiot's game this was. Kenworthy was surely
not on the network of the party on the marsh. This must be
something he had concocted with the wireless operator at the
Incident Center. He put his lips to the microphone.

"Start Operation William in your own time. Keep me informed."

He put down the radio on a coffee-table, leaving it switched
on, a dialogue of mangled voices that might have been speaking
in no known language.

"Within the hour, with any luck, we might have Will Stratton
here."

And after that, Kenworthy allowed a silence to develop. It
was a silence in which no one present could thinkably have
opened up a new line of conversation—except possibly Sally—
and Wright did not think that even she would now risk a new
lead. One of the radio voices went off in an orgiastic mono-
logue, rather like a railway station announcer in a fit of lyrical
abandon. Charlie raised his glass to those few who were drinking.

"Here's to success, then."

"And it isn't all present," Kenworthy said, "who'll say
Amen to that."

Then Charlie was the only one to hear knocking on his distant
back door. Kenworthy raised no objection to his going alone
to answer it. He came back with the Tennants, and there followed the remarks about their babysitter.

"I suppose it was after his own flesh and blood had declined
to help him that he came to you," Kenworthy said.

The remark was addressed to Tennant, but it was too cryptic
for the Major to grasp. He inclined his head quizzically.

"I don't understand, Superintendent."

"I'll reduce it to its simplest terms, then. I'm suggesting